CircleSquare

By Claudia Clarke

ISBN: 978-1-990716-1-0

Cover Design by Tyson Thompson.

Published by:

BOE BOE
CREATIVE

Edited by

Passionate Words
Editing Services

IG – passionate.words.editing246

Acknowledgements

I have always loved reading. According to my mother, before I could read for myself, I loved being read to as a toddler. I would demand that she "read another story", even as she struggled to keep her eyes open at night.

I always wanted to write a book, and now that I have done so, I would like to say thanks to:

The Murrell side of the family, who had a house full of books and magazines. Visiting Marley Vale was always an adventure and I left with a bag full of things to read every single time.

The Bynoe/Clarke side of the family – there were fewer books at Chalmers than there were in Marley Vale – but someone was always reading a newspaper. Granny would devour every item in the paper, especially the local political news. And there were often clippings from Canadian newspapers in the letters my aunts sent to us from Montreal.

Mummy and Daddy – thank you for the small fortune you spent buying me books when I was growing up.

My sister Celia – sorry I was usually reading when you wanted to play. My bad. Also, sorry for that one time I tried to feed you a mud pie. You're the best, and I hope this public declaration will somehow atone for my past misdeeds.

My cousin Steve – thanks for all the encouragement.

Tracy Moore, Jamila Howard, Sadie Dixon, Janelle Ifill, Kim Thorpe – your support and feedback were greatly appreciated.

Robert Gibson, my editor, who provided invaluable guidance on the process of getting my completed manuscript published.

To everyone who actually buys and reads this book - thank you!

Table of Contents

CHAPTER ONE

A Spot of Indigestion/Love, Honour and Respect

Gracewin got off the supermarket shuttle with a slight ache in her left foot. Thank God the shuttle brought her right to her gate so that she didn't have to walk far with all the supermarket bags. It was a pity she had never learnt how to drive but in her day few women had. Then again, what need would she have had for a driver's license all those years in London? It wasn't as if they had had any money to buy a car. Not with saving and scrimping every penny, every shilling and pound to build a house in Barbados when they retired. Anthony had a license but fat lot of help that was. He hardly drove her anywhere but around the bend.

She opened her reliable trolley bag and started piling the cloth bags emblazoned with the name "TESCO" into it. Inside the TESCO bags were groceries from Massy Supermarket. Bajans were finally cottoning on to recycling. It was all a little too late, considering that there were hardly any trucks to pick up the garbage. People here didn't even separate their garbage! They just threw everything in the same bag. They weren't even interested in doing better. Last week the CircleSquare Homeowners' Association had invited a guest lecturer to speak about recycling and separating waste. Ten residents had turned up.

She opened the gate, but before she walked through it, she paused to admire the two-storey wall structure that was her home. It was set back from the road with a magnificent garden that was a riot of colour. Plants thrived under her care. Hibiscus, ginger lilies, crotons and bougainvillea were at the front of the garden. In the back, a variety of trees and a small kitchen garden with thyme, marjoram, okras, cucumbers and tomatoes. The house itself was white with brown trim. A wraparound porch on the lower level invited visitors to sink into the depths of one of the comfortable patio chairs. Not those cheap plastic ones some people had on their verandahs but the nice outdoor furniture with the thick cushions, the type of furniture that you would see in upscale catalogues or one of those stores like Dwellings.

Sometimes she thought her heart would burst with pride when she looked at her house. All those years of enduring the cold in Britain and working her fingers to the bone, first as a canteen assistant in the London Underground, had been worth it. When she arrived in England in the '60s she was shocked at the bitter cold of the weather but equally so at the iciness of London's inhabitants towards the Caribbean immigrants who were coming to ease staff shortages in England and Scotland. Working in England had not been easy, especially in the early days. It was hard to find accommodation, even at homes with "To Let" signs outside. Once the owner saw that the person asking about the room was black, the room was suddenly no longer for rent. It was devastating. Ironically, it was the Government of Barbados that had invited London Transport to recruit from the island. England was Barbados' Mother Country, even if it was a mother who had wrenched her so-called children from the lands of their birth to endure centuries of slavery, and even if it was a mother who did not welcome its children to her own home. But it was worth every insult to come home to this.

It hadn't been all bad, of course. There were a lot of good times. She had made a lot of friends of all races. Some of the white girls were quite friendly and always chatted her up, wanting to know about Barbados and whether she personally knew any of the famous cricketers. Nowadays everybody knew Barbados as an exotic exclusive destination where the likes of British and Hollywood stars and millionaires vacationed.

The day they were leaving London one of the officers at the airport had said, "You're a lucky lot to be returning home to the islands. I can't understand why anyone would leave the warmth to live in Britain."

Gracewin had stared politely at his turbaned head and olive skin as she took her passport from him. Unlike her, his ancestors were probably all born in Britain and had never left a warm climate to live elsewhere. Later, while they waited for their plane to be boarded, Anthony complained bitterly about those "Damned Pakis" and commented, "This is why I glad to be leaving this cold-ass place." She didn't bother to explain that the officer could have been Indian. It reminded her of when their son David had brought home his friend Anesh years ago to play video games. Whenever Anthony saw Anesh he would inevitably start up a tirade about how Pakistanis were taking over Britain and he didn't understand why they didn't stay at home and fight the Tamil Tigers. Apart from being historically out of touch, Anthony had no filter. Anesh patiently explained that his parents were from India, but Anthony would have none of it. Sikh, Hindu, Muslim, Buddhist, as far as he was concerned an Indian was a Pakistani and vice versa. "If black people could look all the same to other people, why couldn't Pakis and Indians look the same to him?" he asked. His logic was astounding and after a while she and Anesh just gave up arguing with him.

She opened the gate, walked into the garage, and unlocked the kitchen door. The noise of the TV greeted her as she entered the house.

"Anthony," she called out. "I'm home."

"Alright," came the reply.

She made her way into the kitchen, slowly unpacked the groceries and set aside the salt fish, corn meal, sweet potatoes and onions on the counter. She took okras and seasoned flying fish from the fridge.

"You hungry?" she said, walking into the family room.

"Starving. I thought you weren't coming back from the supermarket."

Anthony's attention was still firmly focused on the TV. He sat in his favourite chair, the dark blue suede recliner with the shiny patch which looked worn and tired from where his head rested back on it every single day. She hated that chair. It was at odds with the rest of the carefully chosen furniture that James had helped her pick out. James spoke in a language she barely understood, using words like "pared down elegance", "sculptural aesthetic", "contemporary and traditional design" and "clean architecture". At the showrooms they had visited he nonchalantly flung about these terms with the sales staff who nodded and murmured their agreement. After all, James had been named in Interior Design Magazine as a "rising star" in Britain's design world. It didn't matter if she couldn't tell bespoke furniture from factory manufactured pieces. James could, and she made sure to let all visitors to the house know that it was her son who had done such a brilliant job in coordinating the colour scheme and furnishings.

Her disapproving gaze took in the beer bottles at Anthony's feet then travelled over to Ralph, who was slumped in the chair next to the disgusting recliner in the exact position in which she had left him when she went out to do her shopping. Several beer bottles also littered the floor in the vicinity of Ralph's size-nine feet. Anthony's fair skin was flushed, and his dark brown eyes looked faintly bloodshot. Ralph looked half-asleep, but his eyes had a perpetually sleepy look and when he drank, they looked almost shut.

"I guess the match must be really exciting," she said.

"Exciting, my tail!" Anthony steupsed loudly. "These idiots getting paid so much blasted money and don't even have as much talent in their whole body as Gary Sobers or Viv Richards or any of dem had in their lil finger. It's an outrage, that's what it is." Anthony's accent was as Bajan as it had been the day he departed Barbados for London.

"Yuh got that right," Ralph chimed in with his strong Bajan Yankee accent. He had lived in New York for almost forty years. "Some of these jokers wouldn't even make a second eleven back then and them walking 'bout 'pon a cricket field posing in dark shades and can't win a blasted match, let alone a series. West Indies cricket in a sad state."

As Gracewin listened to Ralph, she was once more struck by the thought that he was the epitome of the old school Bajan Yankee. The ones she had seen on visits back home in the '80s, walking up and down town at Crop Over or Christmas time in brightly coloured clothes, the men wearing sneakers and socks pulled up their calves. Ralph was loud, borderline obnoxious on occasion and convinced that he knew everything because he had lived in "Americuh". In fact, he often began sentences with the words "In Americuh". Ralph had picked up his American accent along with his luggage when he first landed at JFK. It was as fake as one of the knock-off designer bags you could buy on Canal Street but unlike those bags, it had lasted for decades.

"Dem is a bunch of clowns," Anthony pronounced. "A disgrace to the West Indies cricket legacy." He finally dragged his attention away from the TV and looked at Gracewin. "What you cooking? I feel like my belly touching my back and Ralph here wid he mouth white."

Anthony was famished and apparently Ralph was too, so Gracewin quickly changed into some home clothes and went into the kitchen where she started making dinner. She sliced three large sweet potatoes and put them in a saucepan to boil. Then she cut both ends off the okras and chopped the remainder. The secret to cooking a mellow bowl of cou cou was turning it properly to make sure that it was not lumpy. Nobody wanted to eat lumpy cou cou. In all her many years of cooking Gracewin had never cooked a bowl of lumpy cou cou. You could call her the cou cou boss. Everybody loved her cou cou. Learning to stir cou cou was a skill that every woman had acquired back in her time. How could you expect to satisfy a Bajan man if you didn't know how to turn cou cou, make meal corn and flour bakes, fish cakes, pumpkin fritters, pudding and souse and all the other things that Bajan men liked to eat?

Today the cou cou would taste as good as always. The okras were tender and not too large, perfect for making cou cou. Large okras were usually hard and unpleasant to eat. She quickly placed the okras in a saucepan with boiling water, some chopped-up onion and sweet pepper and left it to cook until it became thick. That would take about twenty to twenty-five minutes. In the meantime, she rinsed off the salt fish which had been soaking a bowl of water to reduce the saltiness. She didn't want all the saltiness out because that could render the salt fish tasteless. She chopped up more onions, some tomatoes and sweet peppers and then started to make two separate sets of gravy, buckled-back steamed flying fish for Anthony because that was what he had requested this morning, and she would make salt fish gravy for herself. There was enough that Ralph could get a plate of food and seconds. And David had said that he might pass by. David loved Barbados and had relocated a year after she and Anthony moved back. She was convinced that it was so he could drop by and enjoy her cooking.

With both sets of gravy on the stove, she started to make a salad. She peeled three cucumbers then sliced them into a wooden salad bowl to which she added some slivers of onion, a dash of salt and a little lime juice. There was a pear that she had bought a few days ago and she pressed the outside, testing its readiness. It was just right, so she put several slices on a plate. Soon the salt fish and steamed fish gravy were done, and it was time to fry the sweet potatoes. Then it would be time to drain the okras and set the liquid to one side. The liquid would be added to the corn meal gradually and stirred constantly with a cou cou stick to remove any lumps. That part was hard work, especially with the heat from the saucepan rising up in your face. It was hard, hot work but she didn't mind. Cooking cou cou was a ritual passed down from one generation of Bajan women to another. It was a Bajan tradition and a labour of love.

She put the final dish on the table and called Anthony and Ralph. As hungry as they had claimed to be and as poor as they had pronounced the cricket match, they took their sweet time in shuffling over to the table. She took a paper napkin from the napkin holder and dabbed at her brow. She felt hot and sweaty. The kitchen window had been open while she cooked but it was one of those days so still that there seemed to be an absence of air. The leaves in the lime tree outside the kitchen hardly stirred. Turning cou cou in that heat had made her feel every one of her seventy-two years.

"Where the pepper sauce?" Anthony asked as he helped himself. "Can't eat food like this without pepper sauce."

"Mum!" The shout was followed by a loud knocking on the garage door. Gracewin hurried to let David in. A wide smile crossed her face when she saw her youngest child. Tall and slim, David reminded her so much of a younger Anthony. The smile almost disappeared when she saw Tasha behind him. She hugged David tightly and gave Tasha a small smile.

"It's so nice to see both of you," she said as she ushered them in. "We were just about to eat so you can come and get some food."

She went into the kitchen for an additional plate and the forgotten pepper sauce. There was a plate on the table for David, but she should have figured that Tasha would have turned up as well. The woman never seemed to let David out of her sight. Was it necessary for her to be here whenever he came to visit? Gracewin took a knife and fork out of the cutlery drawer and placed them on top of the plate, then returned to the dining room.

David was already sitting at the table, laughing with Anthony and Ralph. Tasha was looking down at the mobile phone that always seemed to be in her hand, her fake fingernails tapping away on the screen. Gracewin had once taken secretarial classes and she wondered how many words per minute Tasha was capable of typing. Was typing on a smart phone a marketable skill like using a typewriter? Was it something one could put on a resume? She placed the plate in front of Tasha who murmured her thanks without looking up. Anthony took the pepper sauce from Gracewin, poured a liberal amount at one side of the plate, stirred it into the gravy, then passed the bottle to Ralph.

"Tasha, aren't you eating?" David asked.

"Yes, but don't put too much for me." Tasha continued to focus on her phone.

David placed two small scoops of cou cou on Tasha's plate with two slices of sweet potato, some salt fish gravy and cucumber salad. Then he dished out his portion and started to eat.

"This is proper, Mum," David half closed his eyes. Gracewin smiled and patted him on the hand. The cou cou was mellow and swimming in the buttery-yellow salt fish gravy. The fork sank through it like a hot knife through butter. The steamed fish looked like something that could be served at a Bajan buffet in a restaurant, with its lashings of white onion and the red cherry tomatoes that grew in her garden. There was no way she was wasting money buying things like herbs and tomatoes when you could grow them yourself. Provided that the monkeys, that were trying to take back the land, let you get any of the produce. Poor David, she felt so sorry for him sometimes, she thought as she searched his face. He looked happy but how happy could he really be, shacking up with a woman who probably didn't even know how to boil water properly?

"Eat as much as you want, David. There's lots more in the kitchen. You probably don't get cou cou too often."

Gracewin a quick look in Tasha's direction, taking in her ridiculously long weave, long nails painted bright pink and smooth, well made-up, dark face. Some of these young women in Barbados were just as strange as the ones she used to see in London. There was even one with blue streaks in her hair on the shuttle this afternoon. She cast another discreet look Tasha's way. She just could not understand what a forty-year-old man like David saw in this thirty-one-year-old black Barbie doll, apart from the obvious. Tasha did not want to get married, David had told her. And neither did he. But what will you do when you have children? Gracewin had asked the question, honestly bewildered. Tasha did not want to have children, it appeared. At least not for a few years. And neither did David. They were too busy right now.

So many changes had taken place in Barbados since she and Anthony left here for England. Impressive wall structures had replaced many chattel houses, there were highways full of Japanese, Korean and European vehicles, village shops had been replaced by supermarket chains and malls. On the surface Barbados was almost unrecognizable but it went deeper than that. Barbados didn't even belong to Bajans, who no longer had a national bank and didn't own most of the large businesses. It was true that people still exchanged niceties like "Good morning", "Good afternoon" and "How are you?" but for the most part the new breed of Bajans was boorish and brutish. They seemed to prefer messaging on a mobile phone to carrying on an actual conversation. People easily cursed or acted aggressive over minor inconveniences. And the slow-paced island life was a thing of the past. Everyone was always in a hurry, always busy although it was arguable that compared with somewhere like Britain, they achieved very little in terms of efficiency and service.

David was busy. He was an independent IT consultant and worked all hours of the day and night. Tasha, like many Bajan women nowadays, was always busy but Gracewin was at a loss as to what they were busy doing. They never cooked and had all the modern conveniences in a house to help them wash and clean. They purchased almost every meal from the supermarket or a drive thru. She saw them at lunchtime waiting in a long line for cooked food, even on Sundays if she went to pick up something after church. Few of them were wearing church clothes so they could not use the excuse that they had spent the morning at church and did not have time to cook. They surely didn't spend their time baking cakes because they bought those in the supermarket. Plain cake, chocolate cake, sweet bread, great cake. She had even read that fights sometimes broke out at Christmas over supermarket cakes but, thankfully, she had never witnessed one. You didn't even have to bake a ham for Christmas either because nowadays you could buy those already baked from the supermarket. Disgraceful. Gracewin's mother, who had made sure that each of her seven daughters knew how to cook every possible dish, would turn in her grave if she knew what a lazy lot Bajan women were nowadays. Gracewin had made sure that her daughters Grace and Linda were cooking at an early age.

"Tasha cooked cou cou last week," David announced. "Cou cou and tuna. It tasted really good too."

Gracewin swallowed her mouthful of cou cou and salt fish. She gave Tasha an assessing look and felt a pang of shame for having misjudged the young woman.

"I didn't know you could cook cou cou," she smiled at Tasha. "I thought you young people weren't into that sort of thing."

"Well, it's easy," Tasha said. "I cook microwave cou cou so it's quick."

Gracewin struggled to collect her thoughts. Even Anthony and Ralph were gobsmacked and had stopped eating to stare at Tasha. The silence stretched awkwardly until finally Ralph gathered his wits enough to speak with some degree of eloquence.

"Microwave cou cou. Wow."

"I could give you the recipe, Mrs. Brathwaite," Tasha continued blithely. "You wouldn't be able to tell the difference between microwave cou cou and regular cou cou. And you don't have to do all that turning and stirring."

Gracewin felt a moment of pity for Tasha and the rest of the disposable generation. Fast food, fast lives and living in a world with smart phones and stupid people. How would these women ever get a man to marry them if they sold themselves so short by living with a man without a ring on their finger and cooking everything in a microwave? Tasha would probably put pumpkin and sweet potatoes in a blender to make conkies instead of using a grater and doing it properly the old-fashioned way. Then she would wrap the conkies in foil instead of banana leaves because she was too busy and tired.

She stole another quick look at Tasha's nails. They were frightfully long, like talons really. There was no way she could cook or clean with those. Could she even wash herself properly? Gracewin looked down at her own short nails. She could count on two hands with fingers left over, the number of times she had worn nail polish in the last ten years. These young women were such a foolish and superficial lot who didn't understand that the way to a man's heart was to his stomach and that taking your time to prepare food for your family was a labour of love. No wonder women nowadays were always writing Dear Christine crying about their man leaving them. So many times she was tempted to write and let these idiots know how to keep a man for fifty years.

"How's the arthritis today?" David asked. His attempt to divert her attention from the microwave faux pas was obvious but she decided to humour him. The poor boy must be embarrassed beyond belief.

"I feel it will rain soon because I am getting a lot of pain in my joints. This wrist is really stiff too." She made a restricted, circling motion with her right wrist. It was sore after turning the cou cou. She would have to rub some Bengay's Balsam on it. "Linda says that she and the children are coming for Christmas. Grace is coming as well. They're trying to get James to come too but he may have to work - decorating for the Christmas gala."

"Never thought a son of mine would turn out to be gay," Anthony said.

"Dad, he's not gay." David automatically spoke up.

"How many real men you know like to match paint and pick out material to make chair cushions?"

"A lot of men do. They're called interior decorators," David said.

"If you say so." Anthony was unconvinced. "As far as I concerned, he gay. From the time a man could tell you the difference between brocade, satin and chiffon and all dem things so, he gay. And always talking 'bout bespoke this and bespoke that. Blasted idiot."

Gracewin's lips thinned. Anthony was so ignorant sometimes.

"You know that James has a girlfriend," she said disapprovingly.

"Hmmph."

David started talking about the recent incidents of school children fighting on buses. Anthony and Ralph took the bait, expounding on how far Barbadian society had fallen. They went on at length about how in their time any adult could take the liberty of disciplining any child who was man or woman enough to misbehave in public and what a fresh cut-ass that child would receive on arriving at home. The talk then switched to sparing the rod and spoiling the child, how privileged and ungrateful Bajan young people were these days and how many miles Anthony and Ralph respectively used to walk to and from school. Without shoes. Then

Anthony filled the table in on Elwood Jones' latest e-mail salvo to the residents of CircleSquare and the responses it had generated. Elwood A.B. Jones was the President of the CircleSquare Homeowners' Association, self-appointed Authority on Everything and General Pain-In-The-Ass. After everyone had finished eating, the conversation trailed off.

"Thanks Mum, I enjoyed that food," David said, patting his stomach.

"I knew you would," Gracewin smiled. "I made sure to put in extra once you said you might stop by."

"It was good but you boiled out too much of the salt from the salt fish." With that her husband of forty-nine years rose from the table and walked back into the family room where he settled back down in front of the TV. Ralph ambled back to his customary position, muttering that he would soon be going home before Petulia started looking for him. That was a bold-faced lie because everyone knew that Petulia seemed happiest when Ralph was out of the house.

"Grace, when you finish clean up, bring a glass of cold water for me," Anthony shouted. "This place so hot that it would make you head back to London. Is a good thing I didn't go out today cause I could only imagine what it must have felt like."

Gracewin looked at the empty plates they had left on the table. Her back felt tired from toting the groceries into the house then standing in front the stove cooking. She slowly rose to her feet.

"David and I will clear the table and wash up the dishes," Tasha said softly. When Gracewin looked at her she saw pity in the younger woman's eyes. "Why don't you just rest yourself?"

"Yeah, Mum. We'll take care of it."

"Okay, thank you both."

She sat back down, mentally looking forward to taking a nice cool shower once they had all left. Then she would watch some TV and read one of the *Home and Garden* magazines James had posted her until she fell asleep. Anthony would remain in the living room watching TV until he fell asleep on the couch.

"Grace! Don't forget the water." Anthony said from the living room.

Gracewin took a good look at Anthony. When they first met, he was a handsome young man of nineteen. They had courted for four years before they got married. Two years after that they had Grace, three years later Linda, James the following year and then David two years later. Anthony was still tall and handsome but now with a full head of silver-gray hair.

She took a good look at Ralph. At seventy-four he was still rumoured to be a ladies' man, which probably explained why Petulia didn't care where he was. Tomorrow, Ralph would find himself at their house sometime during the morning. He and Anthony would sit in front of the telly, switching channels between the BBC and CNN or MSNBC and quarreling about world affairs. She would spend the morning in the kitchen watching a morning talk show while lingering over a cup of tea and reading the newspaper. She would go into her greenhouse to talk to her plants and leave Anthony and Ralph inside listening to one of the local call-in shows and arguing about which moderator and caller were talking rubbish. Ralph would go home for lunch then reappear later in the afternoon to drink beers and, more likely than not, to eat dinner. Then the pattern would be repeated the following day.

She suddenly had a headache and went into the kitchen to get a glass of water and some paracetamol for herself and the glass of water for Anthony. She paused in the doorway when she saw Tasha and David, side by side at the double sink. David was washing the dishes and Tasha was drying them with a kitchen towel. It was a strange sight. She wasn't used to seeing men wash up. In their years together Anthony had never helped her to wash anything even when she was bone-tired after a long day at work and coming home to take care of four children.

"I feel so embarrassed for your mother," Tasha was saying. "I could never let a man treat me like that. She cooks food every day and he can't even get up to get a glass of water? I guess older women don't know how to get men to respect them."

"It was different then," David said. "And my father is, well, you know how he is..."

"Imagine having to put up with him and Ralph," Tasha sounded traumatized. "It's like having two ungrateful husbands. Poor woman. I feel so sorry for her."

Gracewin silently turned around, went straight to her bedroom and shut the door. It was frightfully rude to retire for the night without saying goodbye to David and Tasha, but her headache was becoming worse. She was tempted to stretch out on the bed, but her mother had always said not to lay down too soon after eating. She stood by the door for a moment then sat on the edge of the bed. Her stomach was full. She should have felt sated but instead she felt empty and hollow. It seemed that she had a spot of indigestion. Cou cou, salt fish, pear and cucumber was one of her favourite meals, but, for some strange reason, tonight it was proving to be a hard one to digest.

CHAPTER TWO

Higher Up and Better Off/Heights and Terraces

Stacy listened with half an ear as her daughter chattered on about a party that was coming up at the weekend and how she just had to go because everybody else was going and she would just die of embarrassment if she had to miss it. The stream of consciousness chatter from her sixteen-year-old faded in and out like so much background noise as she flipped through the newspaper and scanned the headlines. There seemed to be only bad news in the newspapers these days. She was beginning to think that Sean was right. Why spend money subscribing to a newspaper full of depressing stories instead just reading the online newspaper for free? Still, she liked to feel the pages of the newspaper between her fingers as she sipped her morning coffee and ate her oatmeal. There were many things that had fallen by the wayside in the digital age but holding a newspaper in her hands was one of the old routines she refused to give up.

"Mum, are you even listening to me?" Rachel's familiar whine broke her concentration and she reluctantly folded the paper and put it down on the granite countertop of the island at which they were all seated in the kitchen.

"Yes, Rache. You can go to the party. Jessica's mother already told me about it."

"Oh my God! Thank you," Rachel jumped to her feet and started dancing around the kitchen. Her dark brown hair was swept up in a ponytail which bounced up and down as she danced, and her heart-shaped face was completely lit up with a broad smile. For a fleeting moment she looked like a younger Rachel who would easily show excitement. Her suddenly sunny disposition outshone the golden glow of the kitchen as the morning sunlight streamed through the windows. It was a rarity to see Rachel smile like this. Nowadays her expression was usually a mixture of teenage boredom and resignation whenever she was in the same room with her younger siblings or her parents. She looked like someone serving out an intolerable life sentence with all possible appeals having been overturned by the Court. The only time her face seemed animated was when her lightning-fast fingers tapped away on her phone or as she reclined with those ridiculously huge headphones clamped over her ears as she listened to the latest K-pop boy band.

"You really letting her go to that party, Mummy? I bet she will spend the whole night trying to get Kyle Haynes to look at her." Dean's voice cracked as he spoke. It seemed like every day the lanky fourteen-year-old was being transformed into a man in front of Stacy's eyes. His shoulders looked broad and manly in his white school shirt. The slight roundness of his younger face was gone, replaced by the angles and planes of Sean's face. Dean wasn't wearing his tie yet and she made a mental note to remind him to put it on before he left the house. Sean didn't seem to notice things like that and last week it was she who had to turn around and go back home, collect a tie and drop it off at the school for Dean.

"You see why I can't stand him? He is such an obnoxious little liar." Rachel's outburst was swift but not uncharacteristic these days.

"Everybody at school knows you like Kyle real bad." Dean nonchalantly shrugged his left shoulder as he finished eating his bacon and eggs. "It's a pity he has the hots for Gina Parker. Maybe if you looked hotter you would have a chance, Rache."

Devin laughed. Hard.

"I hate having to go to the same school as my little brothers." Rachel said contemptuously. "They are beyond embarrassing. I cannot wait until I can go to college."

"Alright, you all cut it out." Stacy raised her voice slightly. "One day you will be glad to have each other." Three pairs of dark brown eyes stared at her in disbelief. She looked at her watch then at Rachel and Dean. "Go and brush your teeth and get your school things together 'cause your father will be leaving in ten minutes."

As the two of them left the room Stacy turned her attention to Devin. Dean's twin shot her a look full of undiluted, 100% proof defiance and she hadn't even opened her mouth yet. He and Dean were identical in appearance, not temperament. Dean was the calm waters of the West Coast with an occasional ripple while Devin was Bathsheba at high tide with roiling waves and snarling surf, constantly threatening to engulf everything in his wake. Someone once told her that it was Devin who should have been named Dean since he had the scowling, brooding look of the old-school Hollywood actor down pat. The actor had not even entered her mind when she and Sean were naming their sons.

"What, Devin?"

"I don't see why I have to get up early like them. It's not like I'm going to school." Not surprisingly, his voice was already deeper than Dean's.

"But you should be going to school and not on three days' suspension. So every day you will get up at the same time as them and you will spend the day doing the work that I got your teachers to send for you. And every evening your father or I will go through it with you just to make sure that you did it. Understand?"

Devin started to suck his teeth but thought better of it when he saw the look on her face. Instead, his eyes blazed the protest that he dared not utter.

"Good. And don't think that you'll be leaving this house at any time during the day. Mrs. Andrews will be here and I already told her to keep an eye on you."

"Don't worry about him. I already had a talk with him." Sean strode into the room with Dean and Rachel trailing behind him. At six feet one and with a muscular body that was a testament to his dedication to exercising, Sean should have scared the living daylights out of Devin with his softly spoken words. Devin, however, looked unmoved until his father stood in front of him and got right in his face. "I don't think this boy would be so ignorant as to do anything but keep his tail inside the house. Right?"

Devin didn't say anything but before he looked away Stacy saw fear on his face. Good. This one, Devin, with his too cool for school, fighting in the canteen, smoking in the backyard, messaging seventeen-year-old-girls self was stress with all capital letters. Sean would soon lose the battle of intimidating his sons and pulling them back from the brink of madness based on his sheer physical size alone, seeing that Devin and Dean were each about five-seven and still growing. At five-eight she was more or less on eye level with the boys. But for now, there was still a residual element of fear lurking around somewhere in both boys where Sean was concerned. She grew up hearing people say that two boar rats couldn't live in the same house and now she understood what they meant. With Dean, Devin and Sean sometimes there was so much testosterone jostling for supremacy that maybe that element of fear was necessary to keep things in check.

"Baby, I'm gone," Sean handed her a stack of envelopes. Her mouth tightened as she looked at them. "Don't forget what we talked about earlier." He leaned forward to kiss her on the lips, but she turned her head slightly at the last moment so that the kiss landed on her jaw.

Sean's eyes were full of apologies as he looked at her. He pointed his chin at Devin. "You. Don't even think about pulling any more stunts, you hear? I will be coming home at some point during the day every day while you're suspended so you better be in this house doing work whenever I get here."

Like setting concrete, Devin's face started to harden. Dean opened his hands, palms up and mouthed "Sorry, bro" to his twin. Rachel shot a dismissive sneer in Devin's direction.

Stacy sighed. Somebody needed to invent an air refresher she could spray in the air to get rid of the overpowering scent of teenage angst.

Bills, bills and more bills. She was tired of bills. She never wanted to see bills again. Stacy sat on the edge of the bed looking at the piles of envelopes that Sean had handed to her earlier. Each contained a bill that seemed to incriminate her. *"We didn't create the problem. We weren't the ones living above our means."*

Except that she and Sean hadn't started out living above their means. In the past, as soon as a bill arrived one of them would simply whip out a chequebook and write a cheque or go online to pay their bills. They were both working for large salaries, even after the horrendous amount of tax was deducted.

Then Sean's company downsized and, unbelievably, he was one of those who lost his job although he was a member of senior management. Even then they weren't too worried because his severance payment was sizeable. Sean set up his own small consulting company in a small office in Belleville. Business was slow in coming in. Sean was a well-regarded business recovery advisor, but it seemed that businesses hardly had enough money to survive, let alone recover.

There was still money in their bank account left over from the severance payment but that was to help get their children into university overseas, starting with Rachel in a couple of years. Rachel already knew that she wanted to go to McGill University. She would probably get a scholarship, but scholarships didn't cover everything, and Rachel would probably want to come home during the semester breaks. As hard as things were, she and Sean had refused to touch the money they had earmarked for education since it was the only real savings they had now.

And there was the house which had seemed like a good idea when they bought it. Ten years ago, CircleSquare was the new "it" development and now it was still a highly desirable area to live in. The name had cracked them up when they saw the ads in the newspaper. CircleSquare brought back memories of square dancing at primary school, forming a circle and promenading. As strange as the name was, the houses were breathtaking. There were several sections to CircleSquare, and their house was in

CircleSquare Terrace where the largest houses were located. Four bedrooms, two with an en-suite bathroom and the others with a shared bathroom, a powder room, a huge kitchen with a walk-in pantry, living room, family room, laundry, gym and study.

With their combined take-home salaries, the mortgage and monthly upkeep were easily affordable. But it had been almost a full year now that Sean was working on his own and there just wasn't enough coming in from his end to help pay anything except the most minor bills. So much for being higher up and better off in the heights and terraces. Stacy felt the full weight of the burden on her size-six shoulders.

Last night they talked about Sean getting a job. There was an ad in the paper for someone with his qualifications, but it was a middle management position and the pay was far below what he was used to earning.

"I can't do that Stacy. I would be reporting to people younger than me and with a lot less experience."

"I know but it pays more than what you're making now. Nobody said you have to do it forever, just 'til things get better."

"I'm too old for that."

What was he talking about? Sean was forty-five, three years older than she was.

"You never know, you could get promoted quickly. The ad says that there's a good opportunity for a hard worker to advance."

"Please. You know that just means that you have to start from scratch and prove yourself. Not me." He had turned on his side and closed his eyes, a clear signal that as far as he was concerned the conversation was at an end.

Then this morning as they were getting dressed, he had hit her with a big rock.

"I think we should rent out the house."

She had paused as she shimmied into her green Calvin Klein sheath dress.

"Excuse me?"

"I think we should rent out the house so we don't have to pay this huge mortgage. Find somewhere smaller to rent and maybe just drive one car."

"So, your solution is not to try to get a job but to rent out our home?" Her voice rose an octave as she pulled the zipper up the side of her dress. "And carpool?"

"It would reduce a lot of our expenses."

"It would also reduce a lot of our expenses if you would find a job," she said tersely as she jammed a pair of diamond studs into her ears.

"Stace, I know this is a lot to deal with. It's not easy for me as a man to know that I'm the one who put us in this position."

"Then be a man and get a job to get us out of this position." She had said the words aloud. A pained expression crossed Sean's face. Stacy turned, walked into the bathroom and started applying her makeup in front of the double vanity. Soon Sean was staring back at her in the mirror as he stood behind her.

Mirror Sean wrapped his arms around her waist and whispered an apology in her ear before he kissed her on the side of her neck. Mirror Sean and Mirror Stacy looked like successful Black Ken and Black Barbie who had been transplanted to Barbados and were living the Bajan dream of owning a piece of the rock. It was just another sunshine-filled day in which they got ready for work then jumped into their matching convertibles and drove off to conquer the world. Mirrors were supposed to reflect the truth, but this mirror lied.

It was already seven-twenty and she was still sitting on the bed adding up bills and staring at the dwindling amount in her savings account. Approximately twenty-five hundred dollars left over after she subtracted all the bills and it was only the sixth of the month. Payday was so far away in the distance that she couldn't even see its head lights. There was still Mrs.

Andrews to be paid, a car due for servicing, music, swimming and other lessons and groceries to be bought. It was impossible.

She had an eight-thirty meeting and at this rate she was going to be late. Stacy went into the walk-in closet and selected a pair of green and brown colour-block Bandalino shoes. Just like the bills had earlier, the contents of the closet seemed to reprimand her. The closet, and the rest of the house, was painted in a soft white. The room felt light and airy and the crown molding gave it a high-end feel. Two sides of the room contained rods for hanging clothes, shelves for more clothes, bags and shoes. The wall facing the door featured a built-in vanity with a bench. The clothes and accessories were arranged by colour. On Sean's side of the walk-in dress and polo shirts, slacks, suits, shoes and sneakers were neatly lined up. It was usually a joy to select an outfit but today the clothes were a beautiful wasteland of excess. They represented tens of thousands of dollars she could use in her bank account right now.

Stacy averted her gaze from all the money hanging in the closet and grabbed her handbag from the bench she had left it on when she came home yesterday. Again, she questioned her sanity as she placed the Louis Vuitton Neverfull MM with its distinctive monogram pattern on her shoulder. What had possessed her to buy herself a fourteen hundred US dollar handbag for her fortieth birthday? That was almost three thousand Barbados dollars. Who needed a three-thousand-dollar bag?

"It's a great investment piece," the saleslady had murmured in a soft, soothing voice as Stacy ran her hand reverently over the handbag. "Iconic." The saleslady was right. Stacy felt like a fiscally and environmentally responsible adult as she signed the credit card receipt and waited for her bag to be packed. Why spend one hundred and twenty dollars on a handbag which might last six months to a year? The average woman had at least two or three handbags in rotation each year. Which means that the average woman spent at least two hundred and forty dollars a year and probably far more than three thousand dollars in a lifetime on handbags that didn't last. She could even pass this Louis Vuitton to Rachel when she was ready. Today it seemed ludicrous that just two years ago she had three thousand dollars available to spend on a handbag.

On her way out the house she poked her head in Devin's bedroom. He was sitting at his desk with his laptop and several textbooks open. Sean had already confiscated his smart phone and if it were left up to her the laptop would have been confiscated as well. Unfortunately, these days almost all the textbooks had online links and references. When she checked the assignments the teachers had sent for Devin, all of them required online research.

There was a spaced-out expression on Devin's face as he gazed out the open window on to the lawn below. He didn't even look up when she walked in. The room looked chaotic, a reflection of the state of Devin's life right now. The navy-blue comforter was rumpled, the sheet was halfway off the bed and the pillows were mashed down in several areas. It seemed that the boy even fought life in his sleep. Clothes had been tossed all over the floor instead of being placed in the clothes basket in the bathroom because that would have been too easy. In a corner, two guitar cases leaned against the wall and various music books were piled haphazardly on top of one another.

"You're only to use that laptop to do schoolwork, you understand? No Netflix, no YouTube, no surfing the net. If I check that laptop history and I see that you have done anything other than research, I am personally confiscating it and you will have to do all your work under supervision on the computer in the study."

She had totally had it with Devin. Fighting in the canteen with a seventeen-year-old girl's boyfriend over pictures the girl and Devin had exchanged was the proverbial last straw. Devin and Dean told her that older girls were always running them down because they were tall and good looking. Girls, they said, had even sent them almost naked pictures of themselves. All unsolicited. It was true that these force-ripe young girls were ridiculous, but Devin was being irresponsible. At this rate he would be a child father by the time he was fifteen.

Devin was silent. Like her, he knew it was an empty threat. He could clear the history on the computer and leave no trace of what he had done all day.

"Devin, you have to get serious about your work. You barely scraped into fourth form and at the last form level meeting half of your teachers were not pleased with your performance. You want to stay down this year while Dean gets promoted?" Dean and Devin were in the same year at school but in different classes. Both were bright but Dean was a diligent student while Devin claimed school was boring and that the teachers hated him. "Are you listening to me?"

More silence from Devin. The child psychologist she had spoken with explained that silence from teenagers was normal and that it was likely "just a phase" Devin was going through. "Engage his passions and be available to talk when he wants to talk" was the advice the psychologist gave. But day after day passed without Devin wanting to talk.

Stacy's gaze took in the state of the room again.

"When you take a break from studying..." Devin's head jerked up at the word "break". Hope flared in his eyes only to die a quick death as she continued. "...You need to tidy up this bedroom. Mrs. Andrews is not here to pick up after you."

"This is worse than being at school." Apparently, he still possessed the power of speech.

"Next time you're about to do something foolish, remember that."

Finally, she was out the house. She got behind the wheel of her Lexus jeep and turned the key. Nothing. She turned the key again and again, and then again for good measure. Nothing.

This couldn't be life. This just could not be life, at least not her life. To onlookers she was higher up and better off living in the heights and terraces. The reality was that she had a virtually out of work husband, a magical "vanishing" bank account, a teenaged rebel son, a drama queen daughter and a dead car battery. Thank God for Dean. So far, he hadn't manifested any personality changes but it was only seven-thirty in the morning.

Stacy got out the jeep and slammed the door in frustration. It made no sense calling Sean because he would almost be near to Rachel and Dean's school and there was no way he could beat traffic to get back here and drop her to work in time for eight-thirty. Maybe she could get a jump start. She looked up at down her side of the street with its well-manicured lawns and flourishing gardens. The garages of the houses next door were already empty. She looked over to the other side of the street, but she didn't even know the names of the some of the neighbours over there and most of the garages were empty, the occupants of the houses having departed for work and school already. Elwood Jones' spotless silver-gray Mercedes was parked neatly in his garage but she would be damned if she would ask him for any favours. Especially since he had circulated that utterly ridiculous e-mail last week.

She started slamming tar. It had been years since she caught a bus but being late for work today wasn't an option. CircleSquare Terrace was about eight minutes' walk to the main road where buses passed regularly so there shouldn't be a long wait. The buses and ZRs passed near to her office; it would be a short walk once she got off. The sun was already boiling hot and she could feel her makeup melting off her face and little rivulets of sweat rolling down the back of her neck where her hair touched her nape. Drivers who lived in one of the CircleSquare developments passed by and stared at her curiously from the air-conditioned comfort of their cars and jeeps. No one offered her a lift because she didn't know most of them and vice versa. It was a good thing that she was in good shape because as she approached the bus stop she saw a ZR just about to pull off and started running.

"Wait, wait."

The van stopped and she got in and sat in the first empty seat she saw, next to a dark-skinned young woman with blue streaks in her hair and cobalt blue lipstick.

"Excuse me, how much is bus fare?' she asked the driver. People in the back of the van tittered and next to her Stacy could feel Blue Hair's shoulders shake silently with laughter.

The conductor looked amused. "$3.50."

Stacy opened her wallet and saw three twenty-dollar bills. She needed to go to the ATM. She passed a twenty to the conductor.

"You ain' got nothing smaller?" he asked.

"No," she said. Blue Hair shook her head, seemingly in disbelief at Stacy's stupidity.

Taking her change from the conductor, she settled back into her seat and kept a firm grip on her handbag. The van stopped to let on two young men. One had his hair in one of those intricate braided styles that were popular with young men. The other had a low Mohawk haircut and gold bobs in both ears. Both looked angry and bitter. Sometimes there was so much hardness in the face of young men she saw on the streets or in the court pages that it bewildered her. How did people who had barely reached the age of twenty seem to have accumulated a lifetime of bitterness and anger that would have been better suited to a disillusioned older man?

Mohawk/Gold Bobs gave the conductor a fist bump.

"Linx, wha' you saying? Sugarland was tight."

"Safe, man."

Mohawk/Gold Bobs, who was apparently named Linx, and Braided Hair gave Stacy a quick once over as they made their way to the back of the van. In the two seconds or so that they looked at her Stacy felt that they had taken an inventory of her jewelry and handbag and done some mental calculations. She tightened her grip around the handles of her Neverfull, suddenly regretting her decision to catch the van. She shouldn't be feeling unsettled by just being in the presence of young men who were black just like her, but she was silently praying to reach her destination as quickly as possible. These boys looked like the boys you saw on the front pages of the newspaper accused of committing some crime or the other; the same little black boys with flat, hard eyes who gave the thumbs up sign while being shepherded into a waiting prison bus, leaving their mothers and girlfriends crying or cheering on the sidelines. Their tuned out, 'bad-man don't give a fuck'-ness was clear for the world to see. It was a look she was familiar with and not just from the newspapers. These boys looked a little bit like Devin.

"So, we're going to Miami for two weeks then straight on a European cruise before we come back home." Kay Forde sipped her San Benedetto water. The twelve-dollar water that would be added to the bill and split evenly three ways. The water had never irritated Stacy before today. After all, it was just another part of the menu at Yattika, the en vogue South Coast restaurant where they had lunch once a month. The ambience was sophisticated, yet the sea-side establishment had a relaxed vibe with its wooden tables and the blue and white striped cushions on each seat. Each table had as its centerpiece a conch shell with bright yellow flowers protruding from one end. Yattika was popular among the business lunch crowd. It was a good place to see and be seen, to eat delicious food and sip expensive water.

"Where are you all going for summer, Stacy?" Kay pushed a lock of her short, expensively coiffed hair behind her ear.

"I'm not sure," Stacy said. Summer was far from her mind. "Maybe we'll just do a staycation."

"You mean like go to The Crane or something?" Kay asked. "I mean, I love The Crane but it's so boring to be in Barbados all summer long."

"Well, we haven't really decided yet." Unless she or Sean won the lottery The Crane was going to be out of the question. By staycation Stacy was more thinking of staying at home and watching Netflix.

"Okay," Kay replied. "I'm sure you'll do something more exciting than just being in Barbados."

"I'm sure they will," Lisa-Marie said. "Did you really take a ZR to work this morning?" Her eyes widened.

Stacy was glad that the conversation had veered away from vacation plans. "Yes, it would have taken too long to wait on a taxi or for Sean to come back to pick me up."

"Wow, couldn't you just get to work late for once? There is no way I would get on a ZR. The drivers are atrocious, and they have some rough-looking characters catching ZRs." Lisa-Marie shuddered and took a long drink of water like she had to cleanse her palate.

"It certainly was an interesting experience," Stacy said, thinking of Blue Hair and the other passengers on the van. Then there was the music, a profanity laced playlist of dancehall filled with the "large-ing off" and "shouting out" of various individuals by the deejay. "Anyhow, the new CEO had a meeting scheduled for this morning so there was no way I could be late."

"Right," Kay agreed. "How is she so far?"

"She seems pleasant enough, but it's early days yet. She has a lot of plans that sound good. We'll see." As the Chief Compliance Officer of one of Barbados' largest finance companies, Stacy would have to work closely with the new CEO. She sincerely hoped that theirs would be a smooth working relationship because she did not need any more stress in her life.

"You need a ride home later?" Lisa-Marie asked.

"No thanks, Sean will pick me up."

When it was time to pay the bill, Stacy remembered that she had less than sixty dollars in her wallet. She reluctantly pulled out her credit card then shoved it back in its slot as she remembered a call from the bank earlier that day. The customer representative reminded her that she had missed her last payment and politely asked when the bank "could expect" a payment. It was a humiliating experience and Stacy was glad that the young man could not see her through the phone. At the same time, she was annoyed. Banks were holding customers all over Barbados ransom with their paltry interest rates, then using the same customers' money to lend to other people at exorbitant rates and they had the gall to be running her down over a late minimum payment? It was legalised robbery.

"The cheque is in the mail," she had lied in her coldest possible voice. The young man on the other end seemed unflustered and cheerily wished her a pleasant day.

Her hand fluttered over the slots in her wallet and she selected another credit card, one that had not been used recently. She placed it on the table.

"You don't have cash?" Lisa-Marie asked as she and Kay calculated the tip, counted out some bills and placed them on the table.

"Not enough. I have to go to the ATM. Totally forgot about it in all the madness this morning." Stacy said smoothly.

"Okay, hold this cash and just put the bill on your card," Lisa-Marie shoved the wad of cash in Stacy's direction.

It was actual cash that Stacy could use now. When the credit card bill came, she would do what she had been doing for the past few months;

pay the minimum balance or just enough to clear some space so that she could use the card again.

Before she left, Mrs. Andrews reported that Devin had worked on his assignments before spending part of the afternoon in the kitchen with her cooking.

"You just have to involve them in whatever you're doing," Mrs. Andrews responded to Stacy's stunned silence. There was no judgment in her voice, but Stacy still squirmed as she listened to the older woman speak. Mrs. Andrews was probably in her early fifties, but she was so capable and efficient that she probably wondered why Stacy didn't have a better handle on her household affairs. Mrs. Andrews exchanged a sympathetic look with her. She had three sons and a daughter. "I let him season the chicken by himself and gave him instructions on when to turn it and take it out."

The cooperative Devin Mrs. Andrews spoke of had disappeared by the time Stacy called everyone downstairs to dinner. Eating dinner together could be a difficult feat to pull off but on nights like this when everyone happened to be in the house, she made a valiant effort to ensure that they put down their smart phones and tablets for a few minutes to actually talk to each other. The other nights each person ate in their own corner by the glow of their respective electronic devices.

"I not hungry. Can I eat later?" he shouted through his bedroom door.

"Boy, get down here now," Sean bellowed.

Devin dragged himself to the dining room table and threw himself into the chair next to Dean. He was wearing a blue Jimi Hendrix T-shirt and a pair of long black basketball shorts. Lately he was obsessed with rock guitarists and "shredding". He listened to Metallica, Megadeth, Ozzy Osbourne, Van Halen and a host of other acts with sinister sounding names. Stacy prayed that he wasn't being indoctrinated into a lifestyle of sex, drugs and rock and roll.

"This tastes a little different," Sean said, after his first few chews of the food. "Like Mrs. Andrews did something different with the chicken."

"It tastes bad to you?" Devin asked.

"No, it tastes really good. Just different. Spicier?"

"Devin cooked the chicken and the rice and peas. Mrs. Andrews told him what to do. I think it tastes great," Stacy said.

"Seriously? This is good, Devin" Sean said. "I didn't know you were interested in cooking."

Devin shrugged. "There wasn't anything else to do. Y'all got my cellphone and tablet, Mrs. Andrews wouldn't let me watch TV and I can't leave the house. In here like Dodds."

"You can live without a smart phone and a tablet, you know," Stacy said. "Or a TV. When we were teenagers there was only one TV station and you had to watch what was on CBC. And there were only regular phones and no call waiting."

"And no messaging girls. If you called a girl that you liked and her father put down the phone in your ear, that was the end of that." Sean winked at Stacy and they laughed.

"Yeah, but that was a really, really long time ago, like in the '80s. I mean, were there even remotes then or you had to get up and change the station?" Dean asked.

"Change the station to what? There was only CBC," Stacy said. "And there was no YouTube so you had to listen to whatever was playing on the radio or play records on the stereo."

"Oh My God. I. Can't. Even. That sounds so archaic. I'm so glad I wasn't born in the olden days," Rachel said. "Anyway, can you take me to the spa on Saturday to get my nails done for the party? And can we go shopping so that I can get something new to wear? Marissa is getting a new romper like the ones we saw in Sheraton. Shari got a new dress to wear so I can't wear anything that they already saw me in."

"Rachel, you don't need anything new to wear to the party. I'm sure you have lots of things that your friends have never seen you in. And you can do your nails at home because you're going to school on Monday and you'll have to take off the polish anyway."

"Are you serious? But everybody is wearing something new." Rachel looked utterly flabbergasted.

"I don't care what everybody is doing," Stacy said.

Rachel pouted. "I always get something new to wear to a party."

"Well, things have to change around here. You all don't realize how lucky you are to live in a house like this and be driven everywhere. When my jeep wouldn't start and I caught the ZR this morning I..."

"You caught a ZR? Cool," Dean said. "Maybe we could catch the ZR home from school sometimes."

"I don't think so," Sean said. "You catch the school bus or wait for me to pick you up."

"See what I mean?" Devin grumbled. "You never get to do anything cool round here."

"You all are missing the point," Stacy spoke up. "You have a lot to be grateful for and it's time that you stopped taking things like getting new clothes and having phones and tablets for granted."

"But Mummy, almost everybody in Barbados has a smart phone and a tablet. It's a necessity," Dean said.

Stacy stared at him in silence for a moment. So, he wasn't the sane one after all. Or maybe this was his version of sanity and she was the insane one for raising a child who could make such an utterance with a completely straight face.

"Smart phones are a luxury. Tablets are a luxury. Do you realize that there are people who work who can't afford these things? You're lucky to have smart phones and tablets."

"Actually, Dean is right." Rachel said. "Everybody at school has a smart phone and a tablet. It's impossible to function in this world without either of them. So, it's not a luxury. Just like getting the romper for the party is not a luxury. I really need it. I can't be the only person not wearing something new." She ended on a pleading note with a beseeching look in her eyes intended to make Stacy relent.

"Nice try but no," Stacy was unmoved.

"Seriously?" Rachel's bottom lip started to quiver. She turned to her father. "Daddy, can you give me money to get the romper?"

"No," Sean shook his head. "You don't need anything new. You have a closet full of clothes so find something in there. You need to stop being so wasteful."

"Yeah, Rache. Stop being wasteful. The only person who has more stuff than you is Mummy," Dean said.

There were two envelopes in the tray on the console table when she got home. One was an ominously thick looking missive which she hoped and prayed was not a credit card statement; the other bore the logo of their insurance company. Instead of opening them right away, she had taken them into the bedroom and shoved them under the stack of books on the bedside table by her side of the bed. She hardly bought "real books" now but sometimes a book was so good that she ordered a physical copy to read again. It was impossible to really curl up and read with an iPad or a Kindle with your head at that weird angle.

She remembered the envelopes at the end of dinner and had stolen away to the bedroom to look at them. She walked over to the bedside table, took a deep breath and tore open the first one. It was the usual update from the bank about a decrease in the interest rates on accounts and several pages outlining changes in charges to various types of accounts. She didn't know people bothered putting money on the bank nowadays. Like the old people used to say, you would be better off keeping the money in a tot under the bed. She breathed a sigh of relief and opened the next envelope then immediately started cursing. It was a bill for their house insurance and it was due at the end of the month. Stacy shoved the bill in the top drawer of the bedside table which was already overflowing with bills. She slammed the drawer then flopped down on the bed on her back with her eyes closed.

Why had she ever wanted to be a grown up? Life was so much simpler as a child. Lazy days spent playing hopscotch and shooting marbles with her brother and sister, eating Shirley biscuits, edges first, so that only the shape of the house remained on them. Eating a cheese-cutter with a red Ju-C to wash it down. Picking dunks and fat pork. What she wouldn't give to be able to go back in time and do any of that instead of facing reality right now.

The sense of being watched made her open her eyes. Rachel stood next to the bed staring at her.

"I was wondering if I could borrow something from your closet to wear to the party," Rachel said tentatively.

"Like what? I don't have clothes that are suitable for sixteen-year old girls "

"That's not true, you have some cool stuff and lots of it you've never even worn. And I need something for the party."

This was probably a teachable moment, but Stacy couldn't be bothered to lecture Rachel on the difference between wants and needs. Not when she was the only one who had "more stuff" than Rachel, as Dean had put it. She waved her hand in the air, conceding defeat.

"Pick out something and let me decide if it's suitable."

Rachel rushed into the closet.

"You remembered that the concert is on Saturday?" Devin asked from the doorway. Devin was voluntarily talking to her? Stacy tried not show her surprise.

"Yes, but you can't go..."

Devin spoke with urgency. "I have to go to the concert. I'm doing a solo. Everyone in class is performing. You promised."

They *had* promised. Devin had told them of the guitar school's concert in his usual offhand way, but she knew better. Devin lived and breathed playing the guitar. If he put half as much effort into his school work as he did into the guitar he would be at the top of his class.

"That was before you got suspended," she said slowly.

"I knew you all wouldn't let me go."

His eyes were stony again. Stacy remembered the boys on the front page of the paper and the ones on the bus earlier that day. Then she remembered the psychologist telling her to engage Devin's passions and to be available to talk when her son was ready. Devin had been practising his solo every day. She would talk to Sean and make him see that Devin needed to perform at the concert.

"I'll talk to your father and let you know what we decide. If we let you go to the concert, you're going to have to do some extra chores around here. And get serious about your schoolwork. I'm not playing with you."

"Thanks."

"Are you going to do that piece I heard you playing on the acoustic guitar?" Stacy had heard him one day strumming a soft, sweet melody which was light years away from the wailing and screaming of his electric guitar. When she told him how much she liked it he scowled and put down the guitar.

"I don't know. I wrote that...it's not finished yet," he reluctantly said without meeting her eyes.

She didn't see this softer Devin too often. "You wrote that? I loved it. I hope you can play it for me when it's finished."

"Maybe." The sides of his mouth turned up in what could pass for the smallest of smiles. Connecting with Devin was a painstaking process, but Stacy had all the time in the world. She wanted to hold on to this moment as long as possible. Just then Rachel emerged from the closet with two arms full of clothes. There was a perceptible change in Devin's energy as Stacy's attention momentarily shifted to Rachel. The moment slipped away.

"Leave the clothes on the bed and I'll look through them later," she said.

Rachel seemed giddy at the prospect of having a new outfit to wear to the party. Her eyes were bright and for the second time that day she bestowed a wide smile upon members of her family. Magnanimous in victory, she paid Devin a compliment.

"Dev, that chicken was really good. Maybe you can cook it again?"

"Maybe," Devin said. "But only for everyone else. Not for you." He permitted himself another small smile.

"Let's go and see what your father and Dean are up to," Stacy spoke as she got up.

Devin and Rachel followed her to the door. As she reached to turn off the light her gaze fell on the bedside table. The corner of the envelope from the insurance company stuck out where she had jammed it into the too full drawer of bills. She would deal with it tomorrow.

She put an arm around each child's shoulder as they left the room. Rachel leaned closer to her. Devin kept a little space between their bodies. Predictably, he didn't lean in, but he didn't pull away either.

CHAPTER THREE

Dear Fellow Residents: A Missive from Elwood A.B. Jones

Re: Urgent - Miscellaneous Matters requiring your immediate attention!

Elwood Jones

ejonesesquire@cshoa.bb

To: CircleSquare Homeowners' Association Mailing Group

October 6, 5:32 PM

Dear Fellow Residents,

It has come to my attention that several breaches of the restrictive covenants have recently occurred, namely the parking or storage of more than three vehicles on a lot, keeping of a litter of puppies, one instance of placing refuse in garbage bags at the side of the street and the painting of a house without obtaining the necessary approval. In this regard, as President of the Board of Directors of the Homeowners' Association, I consider it instructive to remind you that the following restrictive covenants remain in place:

Vehicles on Lot

No more than three (3) private vehicles (which shall mean and include automobiles, SUVs or passenger-type vans, jeeps and pick-ups having a capacity of no more than two (2) tons) and no commercial vehicles of any kind shall be permitted to be parked or stored on the Lot and no vehicles shall be repaired or restored on the Lot.

Pets and Animals

No animals, wildlife, livestock, reptiles or poultry of any kind shall be raised, bred or kept on the Lot or any part thereof, except that a maximum of two (2) dogs and two (2) cats may be permitted thereon and provided only that the keeping of such dogs and cats does not create a nuisance to other residents of CircleSquare and provided further that they are not under any circumstances allowed or permitted to wander unleashed throughout CircleSquare.

Storage of Material

ii) Not to use, store, keep or accumulate upon the Lot any lumber, grass, shrub or tree clippings or plant waste, metals, bulk material or scrap refuse or trash, except within an enclosed structure erected for such purpose appropriately screened from view from the public road or any private roadway in CircleSquare.

Alterations to Buildings

No alteration shall be made to the condition of the buildings nor shall the colour thereof be changed except with the written consent of The Association.

In the event that you have mislaid your copy of the restrictive covenants or are unfamiliar with same, please note that the entire text of the covenants is available online at the CSHOA website which may be accessed with your unique log-in details.

On another note, there was a regrettably low attendance at last week's lecture on The Recycling of Household Materials and Separation of Garbage. We should all be well aware of the challenges facing Barbados in the area of waste disposal and one would have hoped that more residents would have availed themselves of the opportunity to learn more about these important matters. The slide show was most informative and I have taken the liberty of attaching same below so that you may peruse it at your leisure.

Finally, on the recommendation of the Safety Committee, we would like to install four additional security cameras in the north end of the neighbourhood where there are a number of vacant lots.

We look forward to your financial contribution to offset the costs of this venture. We also need additional volunteers for the Neighbourhood Watch.

Your kind cooperation is greatly appreciated.

Kind Regards,

Elwood A.B. Jones

Re: Urgent - Miscellaneous Matters requiring your immediate attention!

Elaine Young

eyoung@my1mail.com

To: ejonesesquire@cshoa.bb

Cc: CircleSquare Homeowners' Association Mailing Group

October 6, 5:35 PM

Elwood,

I told you that the puppies needed to be weaned by their mother before I could find them homes. It is not like I am running a kennel in the neighbourhood. It was completely unnecessary for you to send this e-mail to all.

Elaine

Re: Urgent - Miscellaneous Matters requiring your immediate attention!

Elaine Young

eyoung@my1mail.com

To: ejonesesquire@cshoa.bb

Cc: CircleSquare Homeowners' Association Mailing Group

October 6, 5:40 PM

Dear All,

Apologies. I inadvertently hit Reply All. The intended recipient of my e-mail was Mr. Jones.

Elaine

Re: Urgent - Miscellaneous Matters requiring your immediate attention!

Troy Layne

teeofflayne@my1mail.com

To: eyoung@my1mail.com

Cc: ejonesesquire@cshoa.bb, CircleSquare Homeowners' Association Mailing Group

October 6, 5:41PM

Elaine,

Didn't I tell you this man is a half a idiot?

Sent from my Samsung device

Re: Urgent - Miscellaneous Matters requiring your immediate attention!

Troy Layne

teeofflayne@my1mail.com

To: eyoung@my1mail.com,

Cc: ejonesesquire@cshoa.bb, CircleSquare Homeowners' Association Mailing Group

October 6, 5:41PM

Recall: Troy Layne would like to recall the message.

Sent from my Samsung device

CHAPTER FOUR

Mhizz Iz

I name Izcara but most people does call me Iz or Izzie. My faddah say that Izcara mean "beautiful warrior" but I check Google and I never find it. I even look through a book with baby names in Pages Bookstore and I en see no Izcara. Inga, Irene, Isabella, Isabelle, but no Izcara. So then I look for the names of some of my friends like Trileesha, Chanelle, Alizay and Laquelle but I en see them neider. But it had in bare old fashion names like Josephine, Roseanne and Chloe. I put back dah book 'pon the shelf 'cause it obviously wasn't saying nothing.

Anyhow, my faddah tell me that my name come to he one night when he was meditating, but I feel he mean medicating cause I hear he used to smoke nuff when he did young. And how my name unique and blessed. 'Pon social media you could find me as MhizzIz. Not Izcara Patrick. That is to keep gipsy ass haterz from finding me. But even so, people does still find yuh and want to get up in ur bizness. Why the hell they don't check fuh demself? I doan check fuh dem so why dem checking fuh me?

But dis is wuh gine on. Is Friduh and I gine and get my nails do. And get some new weave 'cause I bored wid dis one I wearing now. Every Friduh I's get my hair do. Or at least guh in town and walk 'bout and see wha' new duh got selling. I dun working fuh people so if I feel like walking 'bout in de middle a de day I could do um. I had a job at a data processing company but dem "let me go". Talking 'bout how I got a Bad Attitude. And I don't match their corporate image. Just because some gipsy Human Resources Director see a video wid me pon stage at a Crop Over fete in a wuk-up competition. Before I could look round sharp de video did gone viral but tell me the truth, dah is she bizness? I din pon dem time. It en like I did in dey when I suppose to be at work. Chaw. And I en de body that put de pictures pon Instagram nor YouTube neider.

She mussee en know dat from de time yuh get in de fete nowadays people does got duh cell phone up in yuh face tekking pictures. Papparazzi. Fuh real. She mussee don't guh nawhey except church anyhow. I tell she I don't feel what dem do to me is fair but she talking bout how I did dressed "in a manner not befitting an employee of the company". I had on short denim shorts, a mesh see-through white crop top and a white tube top underneath. And white lace up sandals. Wha wrong wid dah? Some girls does dress real slack and barely got on clothes when dem gine out. Anyhow, she gine soon realize who in charge cause God doan sleep and He doan like ugly. #offashe #tooblessedtobestressed #Godislove

Well, I get up early dis morning to feed Trequon and put on he clothes so my muddah could carry he to day care pon she way to work. Some days he does stan home with me but most a de time he does go to my friend Kineisha muddah day care. Keneisha muddah and my muddah is friends. I does be glad for lil me time when Trequon at day care. He is only three but could be bare stress sometimes. But before I could get out de bed good somebody did knocking pun de door and shouting out "Izzie. Izzie". It din even six-thirty yet. It did Tre. My child father. Trequon father. Wuh de rangate? People does think dat because ya en working dah mean dat yuh got to get up at de crack of dawn?

So when I open de door, Tre stanning up out dey looking all impatient and like Iz, I Have Somewhere to Go Now. He had on a pair of fade-out jeans and a fade-out black T-Shirt wid Bob Marley pon it. And he work boots. Dah mean he did working again so he mussee bring child money fuh Trequon. Good. Cause my muddah did beginning to get on igrunt talking bout how de chile got two able-bodied parents and none a duh won't find work. And how duh like to bring children in people house but duh doan like to support dem. I ignore she cause Trequon doan even eat dah much so I en know wha she problem is. Plus, wuh she mean by "in people house"? She is Trequon grandmudder.

I rub de sleep outta my eyes and ask Tre if he bring money and he tell me yes. He tell me he working again and he gine pay me fuh dis week and half a wha he owe fuh de week before.

"When you gine pay de rest?"

I had to ask cause ya cahn fool bout wid dese men when it come to money. He say I gine get it next week. I say okay cause Tre en a bad child father. Once he working he does pay pon time and if he en working he muddah or faddah does send money. I know Tre and he parents would do anything fuh Trequon. Is just dat he and me doan deal nuh more.

"Why you don't come for he tonight and keep he til Monduh morning?" Trequon is my little man but I does got he most a de time and I is only 23. At least dis weekend I would get some time to relax. Or guh and spend some time by Darius.

Tre look like he did win money. He does usually pick up Trequon 'pon a Satduh morning and I does tell he mek sure Trequon get back by six o'clock pon a Sunduh evening so he could settle down cause he like he does be hyper when he come from up dey.

"You sure?"

"Yeah. Ask you muddah if wunna got church clothes fuh he up dey or if she want me put some in de bag. Message me an' lemme know."

I shut de door and went back in de bed to get a lil mo sleep. I hear Tre car start up. He did still driving dah old beat-up two-coloured Toyota Corolla dat he had from ever since. De body green and de bonnet black. He so cheap anyhow dat he probably would drive dah til it fall apart 'pon de road. Actually, it did already falling apart cause de second "O" in "Toyota" like it drop off so de car is a Toy ta Corolla.

When I look at Tre I does cahn believe that we used to be a couple. He used to be a lot a sport, did like a lot of partying and would hold some drinks pon a Friduh night when we go in de dub. And sometimes smoke lil bit. As soon as I get pregnant de man start talking 'bout he got responsibility now and he got to mek a better life fuh he child. He start to work in construction and did want me to move in a lil house wid he. I ask he: "Who?" Not me. I en bout washing, cooking and cleaning for no man at my age.

Anyhow, me and Tre break up before Trequon born because Tre wouldn't stop humbugging me...one night he tell me I partying too much and he doan want me gine out wid Chanelle and Keneisha no more cause when dem got in drinks dem does do bare ignorance. Well, yuh dun know he couldn't be talking to me. Dah night I tell he I tired and I stopping down by my muddah but I really went in de dub wid de same Chanelle and Keneisha. We did just in dey enjoying weself and dancing when Tre come in. Some fast ass body message he and tell he I in dey drinking and getting on and send he a picture. Like I stupid enough to drink when I pregnant. The idiot come in dey mekking noise talking bout how I got to come home wid he now. And de men in dey start talking bout he better handle he business and dem woman couldn't be pregnant and in nuh dub. Like somebody ask dem sain. Dah night he and me done one time cause I tell he I en leffing in dey and he tell me he cahn deal wid me no more. My muddah did real vex wid me cause she believe in Tre. She tell me one how I should apologise and get back wid he but I tell she me and he through, finish, D-U-N dun.

I couldn't even lay back down cross de bed good after Tre went long before my muddah bound in the bedroom.

"Wait that was Tre? I hope he bring money cause de two of wunna mekking bare sport."

"Yeah, he bring sain."

"I hope you going into the supermarket and buy some food cause in here is not a hotel. In fact, you does pay in a hotel so you woulda get put out ever since. You listening to me? And mek sure you go in town today self and start looking for work. Is three months now you ent working and you bout here every day watching TV and pon a iPad like a iPad does pay bills."

"Alright Mummy. You ain got to get on so. When I was working I was bringing money in hey and paying bills."

"Was" is the operative word. Past tense. I dealing wid now."

My eyes did still shut but I know that she was by the bedroom door glaring at me. She finally get the message, steupse real hard and went long outside. I did in an out a sleep fuh a lil bit then I feel Trequon jump up pon de bed and start hugging me.

"Mummy, bye bye. Me and Gran leaving."

"No Tre, you say "Gran and I are leaving"."

"You leaving too Mummy?" Trequon start to laugh.

Sometimes he does laugh at nothing and he does look so cute it ain funny.

"No." He was laughing so hard that I start to laugh too. "Don't give the aunties any trouble at day care, hear? Remember you're a big boy now."

"Big boy! Not a baby."

"Trequon!" My muddah was stanning up by the door again. "Time to go."

Trequon kiss me pon my cheek and I kiss he pon top he head then he and my muddah went long. Finally I could get lil rest. Chaw.

I catch de van to get in town. I leh a few vans pass and guh long widdout getting in dem cause some a dem conducters does smell like de en bade fuh de morning and one in particular like to bring bare foolish talk bout how he would like to cah me out. Like he could do sain fuh me. Everybody dun know he got five child muddahs.

When de van did ready to pull off we hear somebody shouting out "Wait, Wait." A woman in a green sleeveless dress and a pair a green and brown colour-block shoes run and get in de van and sit down next to me. She did dress hot and she had a Louis Vuitton handbag dat I swear did real cause she run out from CircleSquare and she look like the type to got real Louis Vuitton not de knockoffs dat nuff girls does be walking bout wid. She had shoulder-length brown hair wid blondish streaks in it. De watch pon she hand look like platinum and gold and she earrings did look like diamond studs. And she did wearing a big wufless diamond wedding and engagement ring set. Dis woman like she head bad cause who does catch de van flashing summuch real bling?

"Excuse me, how much is bus fare?"

The conductor look at me and I did want to dead wid laugh. Wuh part dis woman live in trute? Everybody in Barbados know bus fare gone up to $3.50. She give de conductor a twenty dollar bill. When he ask if she ain got nuttin smaller she say no. It mussee nice to got summuch money. #richpeopleproblems #onlybigbills #ballin.

Anyhow, when I get in town, I went straight by Alizay salon. But yuh does cahn call she Alizay to she face, cause she say nuhbody doan even drink Alize nuh more and she ain know why she muddah had to name she so.

"Morning," I nod at the clients that did sitting down waiting then I went down in the back by Zay station. She did flat ironing a weave that look like de Cambodian straight dat a lotta girls wearing now. Even tho it straight it got body and yuh could curl it too. It cost bout a hundred and fifty dollars to two hundred dollars a bundle depending pon de length and it look like de woman in de chair did wearing bout four hundred and sain dollars in hair. Cambodian straight good fuh when yuh want to look a certain way but yuh only want to spend a few hundred dollars.

"Zay, wuh gine on?"

"I glad you get here. I want you to do a relaxer in two hours and then a weave at two o'clock. And I got to carry Jarred to the doctor for one o'clock cause Patrick cahn get time off today."

Patrick is Zay boyfriend and Jarred father.

"I could do the relaxer but I getting my nails do at one-thirty so I cahn do no weave."

Zay put down the flat iron and roll she eyes at me.

"Izzie, you serious?" She snatch up my hand and look at my nails. "You nails doan even want doing. I done tell Shayla she could get she weave put in today cause she going way tomorrow morning. So try and cancel you nail appointment and do the weave nuh."

"I want my nails paint over to match a outfit I wearing out wid Darius tomorrow night and if I cancel my appointment how I gine get my nails do? You know Gina does be book up pon a Friday and Satduh and I had to beg she to squeeze me in today."

"Izzie, you could do de nails youself or wait til later this evening and let me do them." Zay went back to flat ironing de woman hair. "But that weave got to get put in today cause I done promise the client."

"But is not my client. I doan work in hey."

"Only because you like stopping home. I done tell you that you could get a station in here whenever you ready. Everybody know you could do hair good so you wouldn't got no problem getting clients. You gine do the weave or not? Jarred got the cold real bad so I got to carry he to the doctor today."

She did sound real desperate and I know she din putting on. Zay got she ways but she does let me come in the salon and do hair and when she overbooked she does call me to help she. And she does split the money with me fair. Zay and I does go back to primary school days. It wasn't that I din want to help out Zay but I was tired. I did looking forward just walking bout town and relaxing and getting my nails do. Everybody think that I does stop home when de day come but dem like dem en know I does got Tre clothes to wash and press, got food to cook so my muddah doan get on mo igrunt and clean the house too. Nuhbody like them does doan feel that I does be tired sometimes.

"Alright Zay. I gine do the weave but tell the woman to come at two-fifteen instead cause Gina might be able to finish my nails by then."

"Good."

"I gine come back here in time to do the relaxer."

"Thanks Izzie."

I leff the salon and walk through Swan Street. I look in all the boutiques and try on a few things. It din mek sense buying nuttin cause just yesterday my father tell me he sending in a barrel wid clothes and ting for me and Trequon. My father live in New York wid he wife. He does send tings for me regular and I does go up dey and visit he sometimes. Trequon and I supposed to be gine up for Christmas. He wife cool. She never had children and she mussee too old to get anyway cause she turn forty last year. She does dote pun Trequon and always sending tings fuh he. Plus she does work at a airline and sometimes she and my father does just turn up in Barbados and surprise we.

After I walk through Swan Street I went in the Credit Union. De line did long as shite even tho it was Friduh morning and yuh would think that most people at work. I know I shoulda come in town yesterday. Anyhow, I had money to put pon my account. I do two sets a braids during the week, mek a wig for a girl that I used to work wid at de data processing company and do a weave for a girl that see a picture pon Instagram of a weave I do fuh somebody else. Plus my father send some money by Western Union for me and Trequon so I had 'bout seven hundred dollars to put pon my account and fifty to put pon Trequon account too.

My father is a accountant at a company in New York. My muddah like she does feel a sorta way dat he leff Barbados and went to night school, get qualifications and a good job and get married cause she say when he was in Barbados all he use to do was smoke nuff and pack groceries in de supermarket. Anyway, my father believe in saving money. He tell me to keep putting the money he send for we pon a bank account, mek sure I save sain when I working and most of all never let a man nor my muddah know how much money I does save. He tell me he ain turning my mind against my muddah but she know how to spend what she doan earn.

I doan like to keep money in de house cause my muddah like to borrow my shoes and jewelry and yuh never know when she might find wuh she ain looking for. Dah is why I doan leh people come to the house to get them hair braid or weave put in cause de neighbours might tell my muddah and then she would be longing out she hand fuh more money. So I does meet people I know at dem house and do dem hair or if I ain know dem good, I does leh dem meet me by Alizay salon and give she sain to hold.

When I finally get thru at the Credit Union I had to rush back by Alizay and do the relaxer, then hustle down by Beauty Box to get Gina do my nails then bound back up the road to get in de salon. I barely had time to drink a Tiger Malt and eat a salt fish patty before de next client come to get she weave do. She had three bundles of Indian Curly in 10 inch and 12 inch, so I know she did spend at a good set a money pon dah hair. Dah is wuh I talkin bout.

I did tired as a dog when I finally get back home. Stanning up fuh suh long doing hair doan be nuh sport. After I leff in dey I had to go in the supermarket and buy some things and leh de shuttle drop me home cause dem did too much to walk wid. Dis old woman in de shuttle keep staring at my hair like if she never see blue yet. My hair trouble she? She had a English accent and get off by a big able upstairs downstairs house in CircleSquare so she mussee a returning national or sain. Anyway, after I pack Trequon bag and send he long wid Tre, I finally get to sit down in front de TV to eat de snack box that I buy.

As soon as I sit down my muddah start shouting fuh me from she bedroom. You see wha I talking bout? Yuh does cahn get nuh rest in hay. She did want me do she hair.

"Where you going now?"

My muddah did sitting down in front de vanity so I stan up behind she and start rolling and pinning up she sisterlocks. My muddah look just like me. She tall, dark and slim but both a we got hips and a big behind. Thank God she a lil bigger than me else she would want to borrow my clothes. Tonight my muddah had on a strapless white full-length romper and gold and white sandals. My muddah old but she body still set good so she does dress hot.

"I going to a back in times fete."

Dah is de sorta ting my muddah should be going to. Back in times and vintage soca or reggae. A few months ago I butt she at a fete during Crop Over. You think people my muddah age got any right being in dah sorta fete? She like to fahget she is forty-three and does want to be at Soca Pon de Hill, Dis Is Rick, Machel and everywhere so.

"Back in times and BARP fetes good for you." I let some of the hair fall to the side of my muddah face and pull a few strands over one eye.

"Know yuh place," my muddah leggo a long steupse. "I want some makeup put on."

I went in my bedroom and come back wid my make-up case. When yuh gine out yuh face got to look beat. In other words, yuh makeup got to look flawless, cause camera men and cell phone cameras does be all bout de place. You does doan even know that somebody tekking you picture 'til you see youself online or sain. And nuhbody ain want to end pun social media looking pop down, cause trust me dem pictures does end up all over the world.

I tek my time and mek up my muddah even tho she tell me Trevor gine soon get dey to pick she up. He would just gaw wait. She and Trevor did gine out fuh bout four years now and he keep asking she to get married but my muddah say that men does treat yuh good til yuh get married and she ain looking fuh nuh stress at she age.

I put on some primer pon my muddah face then foundation. She din need much concealer round she eyes cause she en got nuh lotta dark circles like some people does got. I had to fill in she eyebrows lil bit wid pencil and some brow powder then put lil concealer under and above the brows to mek everything clean. Then some emerald green and blue eyeshadow wid lil gold highlighter, lil mascara and of course lil bronzer, blush and a bronzy gold lip gloss. I set everything wid some loose powder. My muddah did on and popping when I finish. She did skinning she teet when she look in de mirror and I leff she tekking a selfie.

My muddah is sain else!

De house did quiet when my muddah went long. I din expect to be at home alone cause Trequon does usually be dey pon Friduh night so I din had nuttin plan to do. I call Darius to see wuh gine on and if he want to guh out. Darius and I start talking to one another bout a year ago. I meet he when I was wid Keneisha by the salad bar in de Barbecue Barn in Chefette by Accra. We did getting some takeaway salad to guh wid we food and Keneisha did mekking me shame de way she did filling up she container. I keep telling she dat de container gine cahn shut when she finish and she tell me is she r-hole money and nuhbody ain say it bound ta shut and nuhbody cahn stop she from filling it up til she ready.

I look up and see two men pon de next side a de salad bar looking at we and dedding wid laff. I tell Keneisha I gine and sit down til she finish cause to tell the trut I din want nuhbody to know I wid she. I does cahn stand common class behaviour. One a de men come over to where I did sitting down and tell me he think my friend trying to pack de whole salad bar in she container and dat Chefette gine got to restock when she done. I start to laugh and he tell me I got a pretty laugh but not as pretty as I look. Men does talk summuch shite sometimes and I did ready to tell he so when

I tek a proper look at he and realize how good he look. Tall, brown skin and wid a low haircut and some pretty brown-green eyes. He had on a army green t-shirt and a pair a navy cargo shorts and navy and blue trainers. He beard did look thick and sweet and I could just imagine myself playing up in it. Anyhow, we talk lil bit and when Keniesha finally did ready to leave he give me he phone number and I message he two days later. And we start gine out the week after dat.

I press Darius name in de phone. I got it save wid a picture a de two a we pon a boat cruise.

"Yeah, babes. Wuh you saying?" Even Darius' voice sexy.

"I good, baby. Trequon sleeping at he faddah and my muddah gone out so I could come over dey now. In fact, I could spend de whole weekend."

"Not now, babes. Remember I have to go to a work cocktail reception tonight?

"Oh yeah. I forget bout dat."

"But I could pick you up afterwards. I'll call you when I ready to leave."

"Alright."

"And I glad you could spend the weekend."

As soon as I put down the phone it start buzzing. It was my girl Chanelle messaging me. She supposed to be name after Chanel the designer but she muddah din know how to spell.

Chanelle: Iz, we gine in Sugarland 2night. I gine pick u up at 11.

Me: I en feeling Sugarland right now. Plus I gine by Darius lata.

Chanelle: I could drop u by Darius after. Or you could tell he pick u up.

Me: Nah. Is alright. I gine lime wid wunna next time.

Chanelle: U getting real boring tho. Always up under Darius. You en went out wid we fuh a long time. Linx gine be deejaying and de got free jello shots so you know dah is bare bashment up in de crank.

Me: Nah Chanelle. Wunna enjoy wunnaself. Lata.

Chanelle: K

I tek a shower and change my clothes then watch some YouTube videos pun hair and makeup. I fall asleep in front de iPad and when I catch myself Darius did pon de phone telling me he passing fuh me now. It was eleven o'clock and I thought he tell me de cocktail party did gine dun round eight o'clock. Anyhow, I en mek nuh noise when he get dey. I just message my muddah to leh she know doan look fuh me and I get in de jeep.

Instead of pulling off Darius look at me hard and I did waiting fuh he to say something. Is the first time he did seeing me with my weave cut to shoulder length and de blue streaks. Alizay freshen it up fuh me this afternoon before we leff de salon and it did look hot. I had on a short blue close-fitting dress the same colour as de streaks so I know Darius eyes would be popping out.

"You dyed your hair blue?"

Captain Obvious.

"No, I put in some blue streaks in my weave. And cut it lil bit."

"Oh." He keep staring at me then he shake he head. "It looked good black. Why you had to put in blue streaks?"

"Because is my hair. I pay for it."

"You don't even need to wear weave anyway. I tired telling you so."

Wuh he mean by dah? Dat I en got picky hair so I shouldn't wear weave? He always telling me that my real hair look good and I could stop wearing weave. I like to wear weave cause is look good and is less hassle than relaxing yuh hair all de time. And um is my head. I could wear whatever I want to wear pun it. Dis night din starting off too good and if this is the igrunt way he gine get on I could see that de two of we en gine last long.

I start to push up my mout in de air and he like he get de message cause he just pull off and turn up de radio.

When I wake up Satduh morning I did starving but Darius start kissing me pon my shoulder so it did a while before we get outta bed. Darius flop down in front de TV and start flipping thru de channels and I start mekking breakfast. Bacon and eggs, plantain, sausages and French toast. Darius does say that my food taste better than he muddah one but doan leh she know. We went out pon de balcony and eat breakfast. Darius got a nice one-bedroom apartment and only six apartments in de complex so de en got nuh lotta people in yuh bizness.

After breakfast Darius drop me by a girl dat did want a weave put in and she muddah did want she hair wash and set. When he pick me back up we went to get pudding and souse. He had pickled sea-cat and keep pushing de fork at me trying to get me to taste some but not me. Sea cat does look too stink. We stan down dey fuh a long time limin and talkin. When we get back it did late so we just sit down pon de couch watching Netflix and eating some barbecued chicken and chips from TNT. I start to yawn during de movie and I did fightin sleep bad.

"You sleepy already?" Darius did sound disappointed. "I thought you were watching the movie with me."

"Sorry but my feet real tired from stanning up."

Darius put my feet in he lap and start rubbin dem. Dah is one of de tings I like bout he. He real considerate. And he bright too. Darius is only twenty-eight but he got a good job at a finance company and he always doing some sorta exams. I ain know how much money he does mek but he ain cheap like some men that does only carry yuh to de drive thru. Darius does carry yuh to proper restaurants. He could handle drinks too. He doan get drunk and puke up bout de place like some fellas but he know how to enjoy heself.

"No problem. We could finish watchin it another time."

Life funny. Once upon a time I woulda never want to stan home pon a Satduh night. Even wid Tre I used to want to be out feting all de time. I still like gine out but it does be nice when me and Darius just watch TV or get something to eat and hang out. When I study it, in a way I still got ta thank Keneisha fuh gettin on so common class in Barbeque Barn cause if she din so lickrish I probably wunt uh meet Darius.

Sunduh Darius spend most a de morning studying. I did still tired but I cook rice and peas, macaroni pie, lamb chops and do some salad. Yes, I could cook cause my muddah would get on igrunt if I in de house de whole day and de ain got nuh food to eat when she get home. Later in the afternoon we went to the beach. I did wearing a new black and white graphic print bikini that Darius bring back fuh me when he went to Miami pon business. Darius tell me how good I look in de swimsuit. I did look good fuh trute, especially wid de same Malaysian curly weave that he play he ain like. Bajan men like to talk nuff rot bout weave but dem too like long hair to touch.

When the sun start to set we pack up we things and walk up the boardwalk. It did real romantic and Darius was holding my hand til we get back in the jeep. As soon as we get home we went straight in de shower to get off all de salt water and then change. When Darius went outside to watch TV I lay down pon de bed and check my messages cause I ain really look at my phone much fuh de weekend. I din missing nuttin cause is only be people messagin yuh every five minutes wid foolishness or puttin up pictures a dem food or demself posing somewhere. If my muddah or Trequon want me dem would call me.

I realize I had three missed calls and six new messages from Trileesha. I ain see Leesha for 'bout two months now. She does work as a hostess in one of dem expensive restaurants in St. James and is a model too so sometimes it doan mek nuh sense checking fuh she 'cause she does be busy. I figure she did want me refresh she weave or something so I call she since I know she doan work pon Sunduh nights.

"Yeah Leesha. I now realize you was calling me. Wuh gine on?"

"Izzie, you see the pictures I send you?"

"Wha' pictures?"

"Look at the pictures and call me back."

I check the pictures she message me and my eyes near pop out my head when I see a picture of Darius wid a pretty brown skin girl wid long curly hair all down in she back smiling up in he face. Den another picture wid de same girl stannin' up next to he in a group a people. She had on a red V-neck armhole peplum dress and black heels and she did looking up in Darius face and laughing. Den de had a picture wid just she and Darius sitting down at a table and she had she arm round Darius.

I call back Leesha.

"Wha part you get dese pictures from?"

"A girl named Brianna send them to me. She see them on Instagram and send them to me cause she said dah look like my friend boyfriend in the pictures."

"And how she know Darius?"

"She does follow you on Instagram. So she does see the pictures that you put up with you and Darius."

I really couldn't remember nuhbody name Brianna following me on Instagram but a lot a people does follow me on Instagram especially when de see my hairstyles. Dah is how yuh does get business.

"And how she know this girl that up under Darius?"

"She does follow the girl on Instagram too. The girl name Rochella Grant. She does bring in clothes and accessories to sell so dat is how Brianna know her."

I look at the pictures again and I feel my head beginning to pound. Darius did skinnin up in de woman face wearing the same pink and white pinstriped shirt and black pants he pick me up in Friduh night. You mean to tell me that this man tell me he gine to a "work cocktail reception" and he did really up under another woman? I tell Leesha thanks and she tell me she en send me de pictures fuh me to do nothing ignorant but if it did she, she would want she friends to tell she 'bout de pictures before anybody else. We finish talking and I just sit down dey pon de bed in shock.

Darius come in and find me sitting down.

"You very quiet back here. I thought you had fallen asleep."

"Oh, I bet you would like me to leff now so you friend could come hay."

Darius stare at me, looking confused. "What you talking about? What friend?"

"Rochelle Grant." I snatch up the phone and push it in he face. "You is a blasted liar. Telling me you going to a work cocktail reception and you out with another woman."

Darius scroll through the pictures and look at me. "Where you got dese from?"

"I din have to get dem from anywhere. You woman Rochelle put dem up on Instagram."

Darius shook his head and stare at me again. "She's not my woman and you should know that. Why you getting on so? We were at a work cocktail reception. Rochelle is a friend from work. She started working at Zenith a few months ago."

"So if she is a friend how come I never hear you mention she name? And why she calling you bae in this picture?"

I point at the picture again. It was straight offa Instagram and underneath she had: "Me and bae had a great time together."

"Rochelle is call everybody bae." Darius stupse like I was getting pon he nerves. "That is just the way she is. Besides, she took a lot of pictures with everybody that night not only me."

He really had to be mekking sport. No woman don't put up a picture of a friend and say "Me and bae had a great time together." He cahn fool me wid dat shite talk.

"So how come I never hear bout Rochelle before?"

"Because I know that this is exactly how you would get on. Igrunt."

"I would get on igrunt?"

Darius start to walk way so I follow he into the living room cause I din dun talking.

"So, if you see me in a picture wid a man hugging me up and he put bae under it you won't feel nuh way?"

"Well, I wouldn't over-react without listening to what you had to say. But that is how you is anyhow. Like to fly off the handle and don't listen."

"Fly off de handle? You tell me you going to a work function dat gine dun at eight o'clock den you turn up after eleven and now de got pictures of you and Rochelle pun Instagram and I flying off de handle?"

"After the reception some of us went to get something to eat and hang out. That is why there is a picture with a whole group of people in it." Darius did talking to me slow like he talking to a child or a idiot. He like he en realize dat de more he talk de worse it did getting fuh he. "Why you does got to get on so? From the time I see how you friend Keneisha does operate I shoulda walk in the opposite direction. I guess birds of a feather does really flock together."

"Wuh dah suppose to mean?"

"It means that unless you learn to tone down the two of we en gine work out. I told you from the start that I don't like drama like all this Instagram shit and looking at pictures online of who wid who. I told Rochelle not to post those pictures but you know wunna women always posing like wunna is models and want pictures online. And what is up with the blue hair? The different weaves every five minutes bad enough."

He like he really lost he mind to be talking to me like dat and trying to blame me for pictures of he and another woman.

"You know what? I gine home now."

I went back in de bedroom and start throwing the few things I walk wid in my weekend bag. De wasn't much things cause I does keep clothes down by Darius anyway. He follow me in de bedroom.

"See what I mean. You can't even sit down like an adult and talk."

"Why I would talk to somebody dat think I is a drama queen wid ghetto blue weave? Dah is why you should stick to somebody like Rochelle wid brown skin and long hair. You muddah would like she and wunna could guh to all the office parties together."

Darius look guilty when I say so. A few months ago he office had a award ceremony and he get a award and tek he muddah as he guest and tell me one how I woulda be bored and I wouldn't enjoy it. I guess I was too much drama and ghetto weave to be round he workmates.

"Wunna men so ignorant wunna doan even realise white and red women does wear nuff extensions and weave too. If summa wunna would guh pon Youtube and watch hair videos wunna would see wha gine on."

I went and stan up by the door and tap my foot. "I ready to leff in hay. You dropping me home or I got to call Kaneisha to pick me up?"

Darius shake he head and pick up he keys off de counter. We en say nuttin to one another and I get out the jeep, slam de door and walk in my muddah house widdout looking back. Tears did beginning to well up in my eyes and I din gine leh he see me crying.

He got to be mad as shite. My muddah right. Come see muh and come live wid muh is two different tings. Men is bare stress. Don't care wha yuh do fuh dem, dem does be some ungrateful bitches. As soon as I get in de house I call Keneisha and link in Chanelle and tell dem de whole story. Dem tell me to get dressed and leh we see if de got anything gine on dat we could guh tuh dah night. Me and my blue weave gine do de dog and bare drinks gine get throw down.

#Ontothenextone #offahe #likehegotinparts #outtoall #yuhdunknow #hennyallnight #cometofetenottopose

CHAPTER FIVE

Feeling to Party/Music Lesson

Leroy wiped his shoes carefully on the mat before removing them and walking into the house in his socks. It was quiet. There was no radio tuned to VOB or CBC and there was no scent of anything coming from the kitchen. He immediately knew that Jen was not at home. His shoulders sagged. It had been a long day, most of it spent driving Mrs. Wakefield to various meetings and then to a doctor's appointment. Most days were like that. Mrs. Wakefield always had somewhere to go, someone to meet, some appointment to keep. She needed to be driven to a meeting of the Board of this charity or to a meeting of the Planning Committee for that fundraiser. For a woman who had no job she was certainly very busy. In the afternoons Leroy picked up her grandchildren from their private school and dropped them home. Then he drove back to the Wakefield house, parked their Mercedes jeep next to their other luxury vehicles in their four-car garage and checked to see whether either of them needed him for anything else. If they didn't, he got into his nine-year-old Toyota Corolla and headed home.

He found Joshua seated at the dining room table with his laptop in front of him. A tall glass of Coca Cola and a plate with a half-eaten ham cutter were to the right of the laptop. Joshua chewed as he typed from a sheaf of papers. He had been working on his Intellectual Property Law assignment when Leroy left home early that morning and by the look of things, he was still working on it.

"Hi Dad. 'Zup?" Joshua asked, his eyes still on the laptop screen.

"I'm cool," Leroy said. "How's that assignment going?" he asked, resting a hand on Joshua's shoulder.

"Good, almost finished. I just have to re-read it for typos before I submit it."

"Good, good, son," Leroy squeezed Joshua's shoulder.

"Your mother not home yet?" he said with a glance at the clock. It was almost five-thirty. Jen was always home by the time he got there. He had been looking forward to his favourite home-cooked meal of breadfruit cou cou, salt fish and a piece of salt meat. Today was one day he didn't care what Dr. Greene had to say about low sodium diets and avoiding high blood pressure.

"No," said Joshua, still typing. "This morning she said that she might stop by the supermarket after work."

"Why didn't she tell me so I could pick her up?" Leroy asked.

"I dunno," Joshua shrugged. "She'll probably take the shuttle."

Leroy pulled his cell phone out of his pocket as he walked towards the bedroom. If Jen wasn't already on the shuttle he would get back in the car and go to the supermarket to pick her up.

"Surprise!"

Several voices shouted at once.

"Happy Birthday Daddy!" Karen said.

"Yeah, Happy Birthday old man," Martin said and gave him a fist bump.

"You all got me good," Leroy said, grinning as he looked into the faces of his family. There was Jen, their eldest son Martin and their daughter Karen. Behind him, Joshua laughed. The only one missing was Lincoln.

He didn't understand Lincoln and if he had a million years, he would never understand Lincoln. Twenty-seven years old, still living at home with no indication of ever planning to move out, and no real job to speak of. At Lincoln's age Leroy was already married with three children. Lincoln should thank his lucky stars that his mother was such a powerful advocate on his behalf because left to Leroy he would have been shown the door a long time ago.

Karen had a job teaching physics at secondary school. Martin worked in the lab at the Queen Elizabeth Hospital. Both used the brains that God gave them to be gainfully employed with a guaranteed salary at the end of the month. Joshua, God bless him, was going to be the first lawyer in the family. It was unbelievable.

Then there was Lincoln, who claimed to be a DJ. He spent several nights playing in nightclubs, the type where fights could break out and guns could pop off if you looked at someone too hard. He came home at all hours of the morning. Jen would always sleep fitfully when he was playing at a fete, and that caused Leroy many restless nights. It was only when she heard the front door open and the sound of Lincoln's footsteps inside the house that she would turn over and fall into a deep slumber.

Work hard. Study. Make something of yourself. It was what Leroy's parents had drilled into him and what he in turn had drilled into his children. Leroy had loved school. He was a solid student, but his parents were poor and when he left school, he started working so that he could help the family. There were seven children, a father who was a gardener and a mother who was a maid. Money did a disappearing act soon after his parents got paid but there was always something to eat, thanks to the strip of land to the back of their house which his father cultivated and the few animals they always raised. New clothes were a luxury and often something his mother sewed on the old Singer machine with the foot pedal. He could picture her now, sitting in the shed roof behind the machine, making clothes and curtains. Everything he was raised to do exemplified Pride and Industry, the national motto of Barbados.

He had failed with Lincoln. Being a DJ wasn't a serious occupation. Unless you got a job at one of the island's radio stations or played with an established DJ crew, there was no guarantee of steady money. Lincoln would just be another of the many young men in Barbados who lived on the fringes of the music industry and thought that they had achieved fame because their mixtapes played on a ZR van or they had a Crop Over release that played on the radio twice.

Lincoln worked at a mechanic's shop for a few years after leaving the Polytechnic. Then he had given up steady, gainful employment to play music. It made no sense at all. Leroy had explained that if he didn't like being a mechanic, he could try his hand at something else once a salary or wages were coming in.

"Look," Leroy had said. "Let me talk to Mrs. Wakefield and see if she can get you a job at the house or with one of her friends."

"Nah," Lincoln said with barely disguised contempt. "Driving Miss Daisy ain' for me."

Driving Miss Daisy? The reference to the film with the rich white woman and her black driver stung. Was that really what Lincoln thought of an honest day's work that helped pay the bills and put food on the table? Didn't he realize how many of his own dreams Leroy had sacrificed to make sure that his children never had to give up their dreams of furthering their education? "Miss Daisy" paid good bonuses at Christmas and had given him a more than generous cheque when Joshua got admitted to study law at the

University. She had a soft spot for Joshua and was anxious to see him do well.

The music that Lincoln played was another sore point. Leroy was no prude but vile didn't begin to describe the lyrics of some of the dancehall he heard coming from Lincoln's bedroom at times. Raw, explicit, overtly sexual and sometimes downright violent. *"Gal open up fuh de drilling." "Ah gine kill she punani." "Buss a bwoy head and leff he fi dead."* One day he had enough and rapped on the door once before throwing it open.

"What is this nonsense you playing in here?"

Lincoln had looked up from his laptop in a distracted manner. When he was listening to music, he was laser focused and intense. If only he could have applied the same degree of attention to his studies, he would have graduated at the top of his class.

"Just some music for a gig tonight."

"This is the kind of music you playing in this house? With those nasty lyrics? You ain't shame for your mother to hear this?"

"She does catch ZR sometimes. She does hear worse," Lincoln said but at least he looked slightly shame-faced and had plugged in his headphones by the time Leroy left the room.

"You waiting on Linc before we start to eat?" Karen asked, bringing Leroy's attention back to the present.

"No, let's eat. God alone knows what time he getting home anyway."

Lincoln entered the dining room as they sat chatting and eating the breadfruit cou cou and salt fish Jen had apparently cooked earlier. He was dressed in a pair of white, narrow-bottomed jeans with red boxers showing under his navy-blue tee shirt. The familiar sense of irritation Leroy associated with Lincoln rose to the fore. How many times had he told him that the 'jeans down the ass and boxers showing' look was not welcome in his house? And why did young men these days insist on wearing jeans that fit like leggings? Lincoln needed to grow up. He was heading for thirty fast and soon would probably still have nothing to call his own except a collection of sneakers, tight fitting pants and a laptop full of music. Leroy cast a sharp glance at Jen who shot him a warning look just as he was about to open his mouth. He needed to have another talk with Lincoln. It was high time he taught him a lesson but he would cede to Jen for now.

"Happy Born Day," Lincoln nodded in Leroy's attention. "Wha' gine on?" He asked the question to the room at large.

Leroy swallowed the reprimand that was on the tip of his tongue. "Thanks," he said, having concluded that a Born Day was a birthday.

"Yes I-yuh!" Lincoln greeted Martin with a fist bump.

"DJ Linx in de place. Hotta than fyah!" Martin returned the greeting.

"Yuh dun know. I playing in Prima tomorrow night. You gine pass thru? It gine be fyah."

"Yeah, I passing thru, lil bro."

"Safe." Lincoln hugged his mother and sister then gave Joshua a fist bump. "Josh, I surprised you took a break from the books. You finished that assignment? I know you getting another A."

Joshua shrugged. "I don't know. This one is a little hard."

"Man, you getting a A. You getting First Class Honours."

Joshua smiled. "I hope so."

Leroy smiled proudly at Joshua then directed his attention to Lincoln and Martin. His words were really intended for Lincoln but he didn't want to make it so obvious and get into an argument tonight of all nights.

"You need to stay out of those nightclubs. All sorts of wild people about the place nowadays. Next thing you hear somebody in there fighting or shots let go."

"Prima safe, Dad" Martin said. "Is a bougie place. DJ Linx moving up."

Lincoln was stony faced as he usually was when Leroy had anything to say.

Leroy remained silent. What was safe in Barbados these days?

Later that evening, he helped Jen put away the leftovers and tidy up the kitchen. A feeling of well-being swept over him as he looked at his wife. They had done well for a driver and a maid who had never been part of the middle class. They had raised four children and sent three of them to University. And Joshua would soon graduate with First Class Honours, and in a couple of years would get called to the Bar.

"How was work?" Jen asked.

"The usual," he said.

"You would never guess what happened today," Jen said as she placed plates in the dish rack to dry. He sensed that she was going to launch into a long tale but he wasn't in the mood to talk about work.

"Mrs. Andrews," he said, pulling her close. "Let me tell you something. I don't want to talk about Devin, Dean, Rachel or the Wakefields. We can talk about them tomorrow. Put on something sexy and leh we find somewhere to go 'cause tonight the black man feeling to party."

They went to a back in time fete, leaving Joshua in his bedroom studying. Lincoln had showered and disappeared before they left home. Karen was splayed out on the couch talking on her phone. She had her own apartment but occasionally she would come over for dinner and end up borrowing one of her mother's nightgowns and sleeping in the drawing room. Leroy secretly liked when she did that although he would make a show of grumbling and asking why she didn't go home.

Jen was wearing a close-fitting black jumpsuit with a low vee in the back. Her braids were loose and flowing down her back, which she knew he liked.

"We ain' went out like this for a long time," he said, as he pulled her close and moved across the dance floor.

"Remember when we were dating and we used to go dancing all the time?" she asked.

"The good old days," he laughed. "When they used to have proper parties and you could enjoy yourself in peace. Not like the young people parties nowadays when if you barely step on a man shoe by mistake he ready to fight. That is why that boy need to stay out of those nightclubs."

"Relax," Jen said, rubbing her hand on his back. "I remember your father never liked you going out but you still used to do it anyway."

It was true. Leroy's father had believed in work and church. When Leroy had started to date Jen, his father's idea of a good time for the couple was sitting next to each other in church and reading from the same Bible.

"True, true."

He swung Jen in a circle as the DJ put on an old Al Green song. He could remember his mother turning up Rediffusion and singing along to this song, swaying slightly as she stood on the spot with her eyes half closed. What she dreamed of he never knew but a smile would come over her face as she listened to Nat King Cole, Brooke Benton, Otis Redding and all the other crooners. Maybe she dreamed of travel and shopping in some of the stores she read about in the discarded fashion magazines she brought home from work. She would pore over them at night when she was drinking her tea and eating some biscuits she periodically dipped in the liquid, looking at things she could never afford to buy, and occasionally running her hand over a page as if she could touch the items. She didn't know that one day Leroy and his siblings would treat their parents to a trip to New York and years later, London. As his mother fantasized about a different world in the pages of a magazine, his father usually sat nearby reading his Bible. A firm believer that God would provide what they needed, if not necessarily what they wanted, he wasn't concerned about travel or new clothing. There was no need to yearn for the things of the world when your world existed in a small house and between the pages of the Bible. "For what should it profit a man, if he shall gain the whole world, and lose his soul?" he often asked. The memories of Leroy's childhood and teenaged years flooded back as the deejay spun one classic after another. He froze mid-step and inhaled sharply, feeling almost as if he was back in the old house and could reach out and touch his younger self, his parents or siblings.

"You getting too old to dance?" Jen joked as he paused.

"Fifty-five isn't that old," he said, a little defensively. Where had the time gone? He already had more grey hair than he liked at his temples. He was generally fit but he definitely felt aches and pains he hadn't felt before.

"No, it isn't. I used to love this song," Jen said, moving her hips from side to side. The deejay had switched to some late '70s disco. "I had a pair of yellow bell bottoms my aunt sent me from New York. And I used to pick out my hair with an Afro comb. Or put it in one with a circle comb."

Leroy and Jen danced for hours, only stopping for the occasional drink or to rest their feet for a few minutes. Donna Summer, Rose Royce, The Bee Gees. The DJ definitely knew good music. Gradually he switched to the hits of the '80s. Each decade's music brought vignettes of the past with it. Leroy was dressing to go on his first date with Jen, after months of being ignored by her. He was at a birthday party for his uncle Max, long gone from this world but for a minute alive and well and laughing with his head thrown back. Leroy was driving to see Jen after Martin was born, the radio in his old car blaring as he raced to the Queen Elizabeth Hospital. It was Saturday morning and his mother and sisters were cleaning the house while he and his brothers helped their father clean around the yard. The sound of music from the radio floated outside. Leroy smiled at the last memory. It was a good one, from a time long before he sat by his mother's bedside listening to songs she used to love. "I love this song," she would say brightly, a serene look on her aged face. "We used to dance to this a lot when I was young." A few minutes later she would look at him in confusion. "You like this music, young man? What your name is again?"

As midnight approached the deejay started to play love songs. Jen's head was on Leroy's shoulder as they swayed to the music. He inhaled her scent, the soft perfume and the feeling of her body filling his senses.

"This is really nice," she murmured.

"Yeah, we must do this again."

The dance floor was as packed as it was when they arrived. This was the kind of evening you could enjoy. Great music with no 'pulling up' and 'wheeling' or deejays talking incessantly. This was the kind of music he would happily pay money to hear. There was something about music that could transport you to another place and time. Tonight, Leroy had journeyed to some of the happiest times of his life, when he was young and full of energy and his family members were all alive. Jen looped her arms around his neck as a Teddy Pendergrass song started to play. Leroy smiled to himself. It had been the perfect birthday, spending time with his children and now being with Jen. Even Lincoln showed up for dinner and managed not to get on his nerves too much.

As the song ended, the DJ's voice came through the speakers.

"Before we take a break, I want to shout out my father Leroy on his Born Day, and my mother Jen, the Queen. This is DJ Linx and I'll be back with some more back in time jams in about thirty minutes."

Leroy looked down at Jen in shock. She looked just as surprised as he felt but still he asked the question that had sprung to his lips.

"Did you know that was Lincoln playing?"

"No, I didn't."

The crowd began to head in various directions, some straight for the bar and others towards the washrooms. Some people milled around on the dance floor or went outside to get some fresh air. There was a small crowd building around the DJ booth, seeking out Lincoln's attention.

Leroy took Jen's hand and led her over to their son.

"I never miss one of these once you're playing."

"I could put in a request for your second set?"

"Great as usual."

The accolades and feedback came steadily. Leroy was surprised at how relaxed Lincoln looked, a genuine smile on his face as he chatted. He was dressed in his trademark narrow-bottomed jeans, this time a dark denim pair with a purple and white patterned long-sleeved, button-down shirt and purple sneakers. It took a few minutes before Lincoln was finally alone and Leroy and Jen could speak to him.

"I didn't know you were playing here," Leroy said while Jen hugged Lincoln.

"You ain' usually interested in what I do," Lincoln's voice was matter of fact.

Leroy shifted awkwardly on the spot. "That's not true," he replied weakly.

"No, it is," Lincoln said with an edge to his voice. "If you can't cut it at school and get eight certificates you ain' interested."

Jen squeezed Leroy's hand as he took a surprisingly painful breath.

"You tell everybody 'bout Martin, Karen and Josh but never Lincoln. Cause I ain' doing nothing but wasting time playing music, right?"

"I...I'm sorry," Leroy said awkwardly.

Lincoln looked pained.

"But you were fantastic tonight. I'm so proud of you." Leroy felt the words rush from him. "Where did you learn to play all these old jams?"

"From listening to the music you used to play on Sundays."

Long buried memories broke to the surface of Leroy's mind. Lincoln was sitting in the corner of the living room watching him reverently remove records from their jackets and place them on the old record player, then gingerly lower the needle to avoid scratches. He would sit there for hours, listening to every song that Leroy selected. No wonder Lincoln knew all his favourite songs.

"I never got to study," Leroy said. "I always wanted to but I had to work from young. I just wanted my children to have the chance I never had."

"But I want a chance to do something different. That studying thing ain' for me. You understand?"

Had Lincoln always been so self-possessed and determined? In the corner of a dimly lit dance floor, Leroy was beginning to see that what he had written off as a refusal to get a proper job was the strength it took to pursue a dream in the face of opposition. It couldn't have been easy for Lincoln, living in the shadow of his siblings, especially Joshua, on whom Leroy showered praise almost daily.

"Sorry," Leroy repeated, wincing at the inadequacy of the words.

He wanted to squeeze Lincoln on the shoulder much in the same way that he had done with Joshua hours earlier. Or rub his hand over Lincoln's Mohawk like he used to affectionately rub his hand over his head when he was a little boy full of ready smiles and gleeful laughter. But Lincoln's face was like rock stone. Leroy wanted to thank Lincoln for the gift of music he had given him tonight, but he couldn't voice the words.

For years he had treated Lincoln like a recalcitrant child, but he was an adult, capable of making his own decisions. Lincoln was right, Leroy silently admitted. He liked boasting about his son the upcoming lawyer, and Karen and Martin the university graduates. He had never really listened to Lincoln when he talked about wanting to be a DJ. It was funny how earlier that night he had been prepared to teach Lincoln a thing or two but in a few hours his son had taught him a lesson he wouldn't soon forget.

CHAPTER SIX

Dear Troy/Back to the Future

July 19

Dear Troy,

You have to realize that writing this letter was not my idea. I would never have come up with such airy-fairy New Age ~~shite~~ nonsense. Right now, you're sixteen years old and I'm forty-six. We are the same person and yet I must write a letter to you, my younger self? What sense does that make? None. It's not like I can send the letter back in time like how Michael J. Fox went Back to the Future in a DeLorean time machine. I used to love that movie. I went to the Globe cinema twice to see it. Once with Anna Taylor and then with Lynn Wood. Remember? Maybe that hasn't happened yet. If not, stop home and save yourself a lot of drama. Up to today if I ever see anybody from school the first thing they ask me is if I remember the time Anna Taylor and Lynn Wood fought over me. If I remember? I was in the middle trying to part them, but I end up holding bare blows. I didn't know Anna used to go to karate lessons. And Lynn was small but let me tell you, she still share out some warm licks.

Anyhow, writing this letter is bare foolishness 'cause you and I never liked much reading. I can see you rolling your eyes and steupsing just like me. I have to write it, so I can graduate from this leadership course I'm doing. Apparently, this letter will put me in touch with my inner self and help heal any wounds left over from my childhood so that I can move forward unencumbered and blah blah blah. All of this is supposed to make me a better person and leader. I don't know who comes up with ~~this shite talk~~ these things.

So, what would I tell my younger self?

First, pick up some text books if you don't want to get Grade 3s in CXC Physics, French and Geography. If you could put in some extra studying right now, you could turn things around. Maybe. I hate to break it to you, but you will also get a Grade 3 in English Literature. This is what will anger the old man the most. "How can you get a 3 in English and a 3 in French when French is a foreign language and English is your mother tongue? How, Troy?" He will ask you this repeatedly for a month straight. You try to explain that this Chinua Achebe William Shakespeare English Literature stuff is not for you. Things fall apart, the centre will not hold, wherefore art thou Macbeth? Nonsense. You don't know this yet, but in the future your phone or computer can translate languages. It can even talk. So that whole French thing is a waste of time anyway.

Secondly, when you meet Vicki Richards, don't ask her for her phone number. If you ask her for her phone number, for the love of God don't go out with her. Since cell phones haven't been invented yet, you still got to go old school when you get a girl's number. If you write her number on your palm, wash it off. If you write it on a piece of paper, throw it away. The woman is a bare psycho, but you won't find that out til she tries to break in your house. Long story.

Thirdly, do not under any circumstances marry Karen Griffith. Yeah, she is pretty, and you think that you love her but trust me, marrying her would be the biggest mistake you would ever make. In fact, she gine mek you smell hell. Ask me how I know.

Last thing, when you move into CircleSquare way, way in the future, don't buy a house next to Elwood Jones. Listen to what I tell you and remember that name. The man is a total idiot. That is the best piece of advice I could give you or really anybody on the face of the earth. You can thank me later.

Yours faithfully,

Me/You

July 26

Dear Troy,

This is still bare foolishness, but they tell me that I have to write another letter as the last one was too superficial and did not explore my innermost feelings. The letter must contain life-changing advice to my younger self. I know, I can't believe it either.

Anyway, people got up in class and read their letters. One woman wrote a real tear-jerker about how she got pregnant as a teenager and dropped out of school at sixteen. After she had the baby, she and the child father broke up and she had to get a job packing groceries at a supermarket. She went to night classes then to Community College and eventually University and now she got a big-up job at a bank. Her daughter won a Barbados scholarship and is a doctor. Yawn.

A man read a letter about how his father used to beat him and his mother until one day when he was fifteen he pulled out a piece of wood and clap a lash cross his father's head. He would tell his younger self that although he is experiencing domestic violence, he will rise above it to become the kind of man his father never was and have a happy family life. I was surprised he didn't bring a violin to play in the background.

After these two letters, some women in class started crying and pulling out tissues. It was like how The Oprah Winfrey Show used to be.

Another fellow read a letter about how when he was at school, children used to laugh at him and call him After Dark or Dark Black cause he was so dark. And how he had a complex for a long time. He did well at university (probably had lots of time to study because no one would date him), got a high paying job and some of the women who used to laugh at him wanted him. The moral of that story apparently was that women like dark black men with money.

Then the lecturer asked me if I would mind sharing my letter with the class and I said no, not at all, my pleasure, happy to oblige. But somehow people didn't think that my advice to my younger self demonstrated the type of "valuable introspection" that the others had carried out "in their journey of self-discovery".

Look, I sleepy right now so I might ball this up in the morning and start again because class is tomorrow and "Dr. Phil" like she want to fail me if I don't write a "proper" letter.

Later,

Troy

July 27

Dear Troy,

When you meet Karen at the cocktail reception, she is pretty and laughs at all your jokes. The mini dress she is wearing showcases her long legs and all the men stare at her as the two of you walk by. It is heady stuff. You feel good knowing that she is the centre of attention. You ask her to dinner on the spot and you leave the reception together. Soon you are an item, and before you really know her, she is pregnant. You get married. Why not? You're twenty-seven and you're in love. You're ready for this.

Anya is a gorgeous little girl and Karen is a good mother. You are happy for a few years but then you begin to get on Karen's nerves and vice versa. Karen doesn't like your job in construction, even though it pays well. Your father is a QC and your two brothers are lawyers in the family firm Layne & Layne and Karen wants you to study law and join them. You can't wrap your head around how somebody who hates to read will pass a law degree, but you have realized that logic is not Karen's strong suit. She wants the life your brothers and their wives have, attending cocktail receptions and high society events but that isn't you. The only reason you were at the reception when you met her is because your boss couldn't attend and asked you to go.

'Come see muh' and 'come live wid muh' is two different things, as the old people say. Karen can whine and nag with the best of them, so to shut her up you start socializing more. It's not what you want but it stops all the damned nagging. Happy wife, happy life and next thing you know she's pregnant again. Things go well until one day in her eight month she doesn't feel the baby kicking. You rush to the doctor, but the baby is dead. Karen is a wreck.

When you get home, you reach for a drink to numb the pain. The vodka tastes good going down. It's just a shot once a day, then a couple times, then maybe three or four times but it's just a shot and you're still going to work and doing what you're supposed to do. Karen is withdrawn. Maybe she needs help, but you need help too. You don't love Karen; you really don't even like her that much, but there is Anya who you love, so you stay. Anyway, how can you leave Karen right now?

People don't even seem to realize that you are a heavy drinker. Vodka doesn't really have a strong scent. You are a fully functioning alcoholic. Until you aren't. One evening you are driving Karen and Anya home from your niece's birthday party. You only had two of the adult drinks but that was on top of the drinks you had earlier in the day. As soon as you start to drive it's clear that you are drunk. Karen pleads with you to stop. You turn to argue with her, swerve and drive into a tree. Karen has a broken collar bone, Anya a broken hand and a scar on her forehead.

Whenever you see that scar you feel like shit. You don't sustain any physical injuries, but your family is forever fractured. Karen moves overseas with Anya and it takes years before you can build a relationship with your daughter.

It takes years before you can declare that you are a recovered alcoholic. Resisting the urge to drink is one of the hardest things you will ever do.

Take my foolish advice and don't take that first drink. But 1 know you, and you will. On your darkest days when you wonder how you will crawl out of the hole you fell into, know that you will recover. You will even work as an addiction counsellor and help others to do the same.

Yours,

Troy

July 28

Dear Troy,

I passed the course. "Dr. Phil" loved the letter. She talked about how I confronted my demons and showed my vulnerabilities, blah blah blah. Some women started crying when I was reading and I'm not shame to say that water started to fill my eyes, but there is a lot of Sahara dust about and you know we have allergies.

After class, all the women surrounded me talking about how they love a man who is in touch with his feelings. This one woman I was checking out told me she thought that I was a jackass but now she realizes that I have depth. She right and wrong; I am a jackass but I ain't got no depth at all.

Anyhow, we have a date this weekend. Her name is Tracie Wood, but I scared to ask if she is family to Lynn.

Yours,

Troy

CHAPTER SEVEN

(Pretty) Complicated / All that's Gold does not Glitter

Monday morning and I'm sitting in the jeep exhausted, my muscles unaccustomed to the early morning workout I subjected myself to at the gym with Zion, who is otherwise known as the personal trainer from hell. Isn't Zion supposed to be heaven or a safe refuge of some sort? It had been a struggle to climb the stairs to the house, bathe, dress and even lift my hand to eat the bowl of cereal that tasted like the cardboard box it came in. If I didn't have to go to work I would have draped my body over the bottom of the stairs and stayed there until I could move.

From the garage I have a clear view of the Brathwaites' house directly across the street. I look at them as I summon the energy to start the engine and press the gas pedal. Stacy Brathwaite is a lucky woman. Her husband is gorgeous, her twin sons are tall and good-looking and her daughter is pretty. Stacy herself is tall and toned, with even medium brown skin and long dark brown hair with blondish streaks. She looks like she goes to the gym every day but with her luck she probably has a fast metabolism and eats like a horse. Her hair and outfits are always on point. And I can't remember having seen her wear the same thing twice. Stacy is living her life like it's golden.

As they rush outside Stacy says something to one of the boys (Boy No.1). I'm not sure if it is Dean or Devin but from my vantage point, I can see Boy No. 1 shake his head and start to talk. Stacy holds up a hand and he quickly shuts his mouth. For the last week or so I only saw one boy going to school. Maybe the other one was ill. Stacy says something to Boy No. 2 and to Rachel, the daughter, then the children get into the back seat of the Honda CRV so that Sean could drive them to school. Then Sean and Stacy lean into each other. They kiss. Every. Single. Morning. They. Kiss. He drives off first and she follows right behind in her Lexus jeep.

I'm not sure why I watch them every morning, but I think I'm fascinated by them because I didn't grow up in a nuclear family. I only found out what that was in first year Sociology at the University. Before we woke up, my mother was out of the house for the early shift at the hospital. My grandmother cooked us breakfast and she or my grandfather walked us to school and back home. My father wasn't around all the time. Sometimes he would show up and stay for a while and other times he would be in and out like The Flash.

When I watch Stacy and Sean, I wonder how it must feel to have everything. I wonder if I could ever be like them, so in love and happily married with kids of my own, sitting pretty with loads of money in the bank.

I drive out of the garage and down the road. Although it is only 7:15 a.m. there is already long line of traffic making its way onto the main road. I turn up the radio for the drive to work and listen to my favourite deejay. He has a quiz every morning with all types of general knowledge questions. It is fun to listen to, and some of the answers from people who call in make me laugh. It is better than the useless chatter and blaring sirens on some of the other stations, the same sirens that make you pull over to the side of the road before you realize that there is no emergency vehicle coming.

I reach the office in twenty minutes and walk inside the building. The elevator doors start to close as I approach them and a man inside presses the button to keep them open. I get on with a thank you and a smile in his direction. I'm thankful that we are the only people on the elevator. I'm not one for early morning conversation and especially not after this morning's instant message tirade from my sister. I hate making small talk with people on the elevator. "Work again, huh?", "I just hate Mondays", and so on and so forth. Luckily the man seems just as uninterested as I am in chatting and we remain silent.

I get off on my floor and flash my access card at the keypad, enter the office and walk straight to my desk. I love my job. I'm a content writer for an advertising and communications company. I help companies write content for their blogs and brand promotions. My job is in a creative field and I don't have to dress in a suit and tie. Today I'm wearing a pair of dark denim skinny jeans, a navy and white polka-dot blouse and an orange jacket. I'm what Bajans like to call pretty for a dark-skinned girl and pretty for a fat girl. If I had a dollar for every man who has told me that I'm a pretty darkie I would have a nice savings account. I'm not as fat as I was six months ago but my stomach could never be called flat. I'm at least still pleasantly plump. The fat wasn't even gained honestly, the good-old fashioned way by eating too much pudding and souse, fried chicken, fish cakes, jam puffs and turnovers. At least I would have enjoyed the journey to Fatville. I eat large salads and small portions of everything else. I eat things that look and taste like cardboard. I even cut out soft, fluffy salt bread with their pillowy fresh-from-the-oven goodness and yet the fat still settles insidiously at my waist and hips just to spite me. The dietitian says that maybe I'm not eating enough, and my body is clinging on to the fat. So now I eat everything in moderation. Everything except bread, that is. Bread is the work of the devil.

The good thing about getting to work so early is that Brianna and Imani aren't around yet. They sit in the two cubicles next to mine and spend all day long talking to each other about clothes, parties, reality shows and their latest crushes. I usually put my headphones on to tune them out. Brianna and Imani have a Mean Girl vibe which is ridiculous for two women in their late twenties. They were openly curious on my first day at work, casting assessing looks at my hair, clothes and handbag. I obviously hadn't measured up to their standards because later that day I'd overheard

Imani remark that while I was pretty "for a dark-skinned girl" I needed to lose "like thirty pounds". Brianna and Imani are slim with flat stomachs, the type of girls who would never have allowed even five extra pounds to take up temporary residence on their person. They don't like me (boohoo), and I don't like them.

The morning passes quickly and soon it's time for lunch. I take the elevator down to the main lunchroom which is shared by all the offices in the building. Our office also has its own tiny lunchroom, and while I don't have to use the main lunchroom, I like to. It is a chance to get away from my colleagues and see some other people. I can also just sit at a table in the back by myself and read without having to make conversation with anyone.

I'm eating my lunch of quinoa (ugh), broiled snapper and roasted vegetables and catching up on some of my favorite blogs on my phone when I hear someone speaking to me.

Without looking up I know it's Brandon. Since I started working here about six months ago, I've bumped into him from time to time. He works in the IT department in one of the companies in the building. He's popular with the ladies. Whenever I see him there always seems to be some woman chatting with him or laughing at something he said. Brandon is one of the reasons Brianna and Imani don't like me, although I hardly know him. Based on some snippets of a conversation I overheard between those two, he pretty much ignores them. He and some other guys have a side hustle running a business which holds fetes at Crop Over and other times, and despite their persistence in showing up at every event, Brianna and Imani still haven't managed to get the time of day from him. They saw us eating lunch at the same table once and when I went back to my desk tried their best to find out from me if I'd known him before. It was obviously the only reason he would have had for talking to me, right? I had just met him a few minutes before they came into the lunchroom. It was a Monday and the lunchroom was packed since almost everyone had leftovers from the weekend. He was looking around for an empty space to sit when his eyes landed on the vacant seat next to me at the table for two.

"Is this seat taken?" It is the same question he asks now.

Just like I did that first time we met, I say "No" and continue reading on my phone. I'm not trying to be rude, but I really like to relax at lunch by reading or watching a movie. I have no problem with anyone eating lunch next to me once they don't expect me to carry on a conversation. Luckily most people in the lunchroom, like me, are more interested in their food and phones than anything else. Brandon is no different, the few times we've eaten at the same table he has only carried on the most perfunctory conversation before pulling out his phone.

"Had a good weekend?" he asks.

"Yeah. You?"

"Yeah, busy but good."

"Cool," I say. We eat and read in silence until a quick glance at my watch confirms that my lunch hour will be up in ten minutes. My muscles protest when I stand up and a small groan escapes my lips.

"Are you okay?" Brandon looks up.

"Yeah," I respond. "Just sore from the gym." I don't know why I volunteered the information but maybe the fact that he doesn't try to force conversation has made me more inclined to be a little friendlier to him.

"Which gym do you go to?"

"LifeForce."

It's obvious that he exercises a lot. He's a good-looking guy, not drop-dead gorgeous, but it's his body that is a work of art. His broad shoulders fill out his shirt just right and his flat stomach hints at washboard abs.

"Hey, I go there too," he says excitedly. "If you ever need a workout partner let me know."

"Thanks, but I have a trainer," I say self-consciously, uncomfortable at the thought of being anywhere near to him in workout clothes showcasing my extra pounds. I hope that I never run into him at the gym. "I really have to get back to my desk." I quickly change the topic.

"Already?" He holds out his hand. "Give me your phone."

I hand it to him, confused. He types in something then passes it back to me.

"Now you have my number and I have yours," he says. "If your trainer isn't available, you can hit me up."

I'm not sure what is happening. I know I'm pretty and I know I dress well. I'm not insecure because people are stupid enough to try that pretty "for a dark girl" or "for a fat girl" crap. But Brandon clearly could never be hitting on me because I'm not the type guys like him check for. He must be one of those people who makes friends easily and reaches out to people.

"Great," I say. "See you around."

Surprise, surprise. Not. Although I told her I would be there at six o'clock my sister is nowhere to be found when I arrive at my mother's house. However, when I walk into the dining room someone who I haven't seen in about six years is sitting at the table eating a plate of food as calmly as you please. I blink and look again, certain that my eyes must be deceiving me, but it's true. My father, wearing a navy-blue t-shirt and a pair of boxer shorts, is yamming a plate of rice and stew.

I stare at my mother in disbelief, but she quickly looks away and keeps her eyes focused on her plate. My youngest brother Nicky is sitting at the table eating with them and chattering away with my parents. Jalia and Jalicia are also there, laughing at some story that Nicky is recounting and piping in at intervals. It all looks very familial and cosy, but I want to pull my mother aside and ask her what the hell is going on. The food looks so good that my stomach rumbles loudly, reminding me that I haven't eaten since my two o'clock snack.

"You want something to eat?" my mother asks.

I say no. I'm supposed to eat every three hours, but I no longer eat white rice. I could eat the stew and some of the salad, but I really don't feel like playing whatever this latest game of my father's is.

I walk over to where Nicky is sitting and hug him. "Nicky boo," I say. "How you doing?"

"Fine," he hugs me back distractedly then turns back to talk to our father. Jalia and Jalicia are more welcoming and shower me with kisses while they listen to Nicky. I sit next to them at the opposite end of the table to him. They all laugh when Nicky finishes talking.

My father says, "That was really funny, Nicky." My brother preens from the attention.

"Faye," my father says. "You look well. How are things going?"

He has the nerve to speak to me as if I'm someone who he sees regularly. If he had wanted to know how things were going, he would have found time to come around and ask a question in the last six years. I start to suck my teeth but decide to just ignore him.

"Where's Alicia?" I ask.

"She said to tell you that she running 'bout half an hour late," my mother says.

"Is Dante here?" I ask.

"In the back," my mother says.

I get up from the table and walk towards the back of the house. Although I lived here up to a year ago, I'm surprised at how cramped it feels whenever I visit. The three bedrooms and one bathroom had always felt over-crowded with four adults and three children. Now that I'm accustomed to living at Auntie Niya's, my mother's house feels claustrophobic. Here, nobody has his own bedroom. The study is the dining room table and the laundry room is the sink and washing machine outside in the yard. The family room is everywhere because here you can't escape family so there is no need for a designated room where people can gather. There is never a moment of solitude in here. Someone is always sucking up the oxygen and silence, vying with your thoughts for attention. There is no space to have space.

"Dante," I raise my voice. I knock on his bedroom door and wait until he shouts for me to enter. Dante is twenty-two. He works and studies mechanics part-time at the Polytechnic.

"What is he doing here?" I ask angrily.

Dante looks up from his position on the bed. He is resting against the headboard, wearing a t-shirt and a pair of track suit bottoms, with a book open on his lap. I'm so upset I don't even feel guilty for interrupting his studying.

"What it look like he doing?" he asks calmly.

Sometimes Dante is so zen that it drives me insane.

"It looks like he's eating dinner," I say slowly, making quotation marks in the air as I draw out the word "looks".

"But what is he doing here?"

Dante shoots me an unperturbed look. "You ain going like the answer I give you."

"Is he living here?" My voice rises on the back end of my question.

Unlike my mother, Dante doesn't back down from the anger in my gaze.

"Yeah."

"Shit!" This is unfuckingbelievable. "How long has he been here?" I ask.

"He started coming around a few months ago," Dante is still cool.

"A few months? But I've been here almost every weekend to see Nicky and the girls. I've never seen him once." I'm totally bewildered.

"I guess he wasn't here then." Dante shrugs.

I look around the bedroom Dante and Nicky share and bite my lip to keep from exploding. The room, while small, is bright and airy. The walls are painted a soft cream. I remember the day I brought the paint home. Soft cream for the bedrooms, pale blue for the bathroom and a pretty peach for the living room and dining room. Dante, Alicia and I spent an entire weekend sprucing up the house. That was three years ago, and it still looks pretty good. Even for a room occupied by two people with Y chromosomes, it is tidy. It once used to look like a hot mess, clothes thrown on the pegs protruding from a piece of board nailed to the back on the door or bulging out of the drawers of a sagging, too-stuffed chest of drawers which used to be in a corner of the room. Now, their clothes are neatly packed away in a large wardrobe I took out on hire purchase once I started to work. Books are stacked tidily on a small desk in the corner, and a small laptop is next to the books. My money has helped to pay for almost everything in the room.

"Hey," Dante says, drawing me out of my thoughts. "I knew you would get upset but is her house. And he's not bad. Nicky and the girls like having him around."

I stare at him wordlessly. I'm actually incapable of speech.

I leave the room. I'll have to catch up with Alicia another time but it's her fault for not being around. When I go back to the dining room it is empty. I follow the sound of voices into the living room. Everyone is sitting in front of the television watching something on the Cartoon Network. My father is stretched out on the couch I finished paying for last year, with his feet propped up on the same coffee table that my mother would tar and feather anyone else for using as a pouffe. Nicky is sitting between him and my mother. Jalicia and Jalia are on two throw cushions on the ground.

I look at them like I'm watching a movie with people I don't know. Nicky looks the happiest I have ever seen him. My mother looks tired and overworked, as usual, but the lines around her eyes and mouth seem softer. She's laughing again. I've heard her laugh more this evening than I have in years. My father's arm is stretched out along the back of the sofa, resting on her shoulder.

"Nicky, Jalicia, Jalia, I'll see you at the weekend," I speak from the doorway.

"Okay Faye, but Daddy taking us to the cinema on Saturday afternoon so don't come then."

"Okay," I reply to Nicky while staring at my father.

Memories of all the times my father said he would take Dante, Alicia or me somewhere and never showed up flash across my mind. I already feel for Nicky and the girls.

I hear footsteps following me as I make my way back out the house through the dining room.

"Faye." My mother's voice is soft. "I should have told you your father was back."

The word "back" is funny, almost as funny as "father". I try not to laugh. It sounds like he was on a mission to Mars or somewhere. I have nothing to say so I pick up my handbag from where I had left it on a dining room chair and sling it over my shoulder.

"You wouldn't understand," she says pleadingly. "Maybe one of these days when you find somebody..." Her voice trails off at the look on my face.

This isn't the first time my father has pulled this moving back into the house stunt. The last time was when Nicky, who is eleven now, was little, but I still know how this will turn out.

"I can't believe you would do this to Nicky," I say tightly. "Or to the girls. What is going to happen to them when he leaves again?"

My father enters the room and stands next to my mother as if she needs to be protected from me instead of from herself. How can one woman be so weak? How can she let him back in so easily?

"I'm not leaving again. No matter what, I'll be here for all of you."

He stares me down. I stare back.

"I'm sorry for being such a poor father. I'm going to do better."

There is an earnest expression on his face. His words sound good, but I don't believe him. My father is a confidence man who gambles with hearts instead of money; a three-card man who tricks you into thinking that you know which card is which when in fact you know nothing.

I take a good look at Nicholas Dante Peters. He has aged well and looks good for a man in his mid-fifties. He's charismatic and can be hilarious. I remember him telling us the funniest jokes and jumping out from the most unlikely places when we played hide and seek. He was a great storyteller;

probably still is, since having an easy explanation for why he didn't do what he said he was going to do always seemed to come to him so easily. I look at him and I see Dante and Nicky. They have the same medium brown skin, wide set eyes and lopsided grin. Even their hair is the same texture although my father's short, thick Afro is sprinkled with a little grey while Dante has a low mohawk which Nicky also gets during the summer. It is too late for my father to do better by me and I feel sorry for anyone foolish enough to expect him to deliver on these new promises. He's like a Bajan politician at election time. Promises, promises, promises. And later, broken promises for days. I walk out the door and get into Aunt Niya's jeep. As I'm about to turn the engine on I hear Dante calling my name. He rushes outside and leans into the open driver's window.

"Hey, Alicia tell you she gine be here in two minutes so not to leave."

Dante gets into the passenger seat, so I know he wants to talk. I take a gluten free, taste free energy bar out of my handbag and start to eat it. I remember the smell of the rice and stew the others were eating. I miss my mother's cooking. She is such a good cook and her rice and stew smells like home.

Truthfully, I don't want to hear anything that Dante has to say. I can't believe that my father, who has not sent one red cent to support his family over the past few years, has just turned up and walked into the open arms of everyone. I skimped and saved for the last few years with my mother to make sure that they were comfortable. The way I treat Jalicia and Jalia you would think that they are my daughters, not my nieces. And yet no-one, not my mother, Alicia or Dante, saw fit to tell me that he was back.

"I think he's trying. We talk a lot and he gives me advice about studying and not messing up my life like he messed up his. You should spend some time with him. He bought some blocks and material and some men coming on Saturday to start working on another bathroom and bedroom."

"I see."

There is a loud rumble in the road. A small orange car screeches to a halt in front of my mother's house and out hops Alicia, dressed in a tight red and navy dress. The front is cut low and the tops of her breasts appear to be trying to escape from the flimsy material. She leans into the car to give whoever is dropping her home an eyeful. When she turns to walk away, the driver does not move off immediately. It is still light enough outside for me to see him staring at her behind.

"Yeah, Faye," Alicia leans against the door of the jeep. Since I last saw her she has cut her hair into a low texturized afro and dyed it a dark blonde. It suits her. "You got the thing I ask you for?"

I silently hand her an envelope with two hundred dollars in it. I'm tired of Alicia always begging for money. She claims that it's for some undisclosed important reason but if I know my sister, she probably needs a new outfit to wear to a fete.

"Thanks," she takes the envelope and continues towards the house. A pang of guilt seems to prick her. "You good?" she half turns and waits for my nod before walking on.

"Daddy told her she has to get a job," Dante says. "The money is to buy something to wear to interviews because he told her that everything she owns is too tight."

It's so good to be back at Aunt Niya's house after all the madness that went down earlier that afternoon. I take a long shower with some of the expensive shower gel she gave me last Christmas, the one I keep for special occasions. Aunt Niya has always been a lifesaver for me. She isn't even related to us. She and my mother have been friends since they grew up together in the same village my mother still lives in. Aunt Niya is a senior executive in a large insurance company and has no children of her own. She's glamorous, well-educated and well paid. She's generous and really helped us out when my father left for the last time. I could never have gone to university without her help. When I got my first job, she took me shopping and paid for everything.

I turn off the shower and walk out of the en-suite bathroom into the bedroom. Every one of the three bedrooms in the house has a bathroom en suite. Aunt Niya's bedroom even has a small sitting area. I'm using one of the guest bedrooms while I house-sit and it feels as peaceful and serene as a hotel room, not that I've been in many.

I quickly towel-dry myself and apply lotion to my body before I put on my comfiest pair of pajamas and a pair of socks. It's February and the nights are still chilly. I go downstairs in search of something to eat and end up warming up some leftover chicken and vegetables from the weekend. I curl up on the couch in front of the TV in the family room and eat my dinner slowly while I watch the entertainment news.

After I eat, I stretch out on top of the throw I keep draped over the couch and watch a movie on Netflix. I'm very careful to keep Aunt Niya's things in pristine condition. I couldn't believe it when she told me she was going to be heading up a new business unit in St. Lucia for a year and wanted me to house sit for her. It was a chance to get some space and time to myself without having to find money I couldn't afford to pay for an apartment.

I find my thoughts straying back to earlier that evening. My father is back. My grandmother had to have known. She and my grandfather live close to my mother and usually visit her a few times a week.

Asking my grandmother anything would be a waste of time. "*Stay out of big people's business.*" It was a favourite line of hers. Aunt Niya would be no better. "*You need to live a little, Faye. Stop taking on everybody's life* decisions as your own. Let Alicia mind her own children instead of going out every weekend while you stay at home... Do you even go out on dates?" She had shot a barrage of questions at me when I told her that I couldn't abandon Nicky and the girls to house sit for her.

"Sometimes," I had replied vaguely.

They probably all knew my father was back and decided not to tell me anything. I'm in such a bad mood that I decide to eat a piece of the chocolate bar I keep in the fridge for truly desperate moments. As I'm getting off the couch my phone buzzes and I look down to see that there is a message from Brandon. At first, I am confused then I remember that he put his number in my phone at lunch time.

Hey, when do you usually go to the gym?

Early morning.

How early is early?

We start messaging back and forth. I forget about the chocolate and soon I am curled back up on the couch with a smile on my face. It turns out that Brandon usually goes to the gym after work, so the chances of our paths crossing are slim to non-existent. Perfect.

At first, I am wary about why he is being so nice, and my responses are almost curt. Is he feeling sorry for me because I need to lose weight? Am I a Help the Fat Girl Project he has adopted? When you're overweight people always have "helpful" unsolicited advice about how you should lose weight. Drink this, eat that, don't eat that, exercise more...it never ends. He doesn't come across that way as we message, though. In fact, we only message about the gym for a few minutes then start discussing everything under the sun. Movies, work, music, politics. For the next hour or so we talk about it all. Then my eyes begin to get droopy and I'm on the verge of typing gibberish so I reluctantly tell Brandon that I'm going to bed. I fall asleep on the couch with a smile on my lips. I don't know the last time I laughed so much. He's so funny that he reminds me of my father who used to make me laugh when I was growing up with all his jokes and non-stop tickling. Then, when I was a teenager, we would watch all the latest comedies and laugh nonstop. For days after my father would act out certain scenes or lines and we would laugh again. In those days I was so happy to see him that I welcomed him back every time he drifted in and out of our lives. But that was a lifetime ago and as I fall to sleep I am thinking about how cool Brandon is and how cute he looks in his profile picture. My father is far, far from my mind.

I end up eating lunch with Brandon almost every day for the rest of the week. Around lunchtime on Tuesday he messages me saying he is going to the cafeteria in ten minutes and will save a seat for me. Brianna and Imani have been working my nerves for the entire morning, so I'm happy to have someone friendly to hang out with at lunch time. We chat a little but then we eat in silence while I read on my phone and he watches a movie on his. This is how it is for most of the week except for one day when I am out to a client meeting. On Friday as we pack up our things at the end of lunch, Brandon asks casually "You wanna catch that movie tomorrow night?"

He's talking about the latest Marvel movie. During one of our numerous chats, we discovered that we both love the Marvel Cinematic Universe. A little ball of excitement starts to roll around in my stomach. I can't believe it, but I like Brandon. I like him *like him*. And now he is asking me out. We get along well and he's always saying something to make me laugh. We message each other a lot, so much so that I have to be careful not to check my phone around Brianna and Imani because I know I will start smiling when I look down and see a message from him. I can't risk that even though I am here trying not to grin like a fool in the middle of the lunchroom. Just as I am about to open my mouth to let him know I would like to see the movie, two girls I vaguely recognize from one of the other offices in the building walk up and start talking to him. They totally ignore me, like I am invisible or something.

"Soooo, Brandon," the first girl says, flipping what looks like several yards of weave over her shoulder. "You still hooking us up with the passes for tonight, right?"

"Yeah, just check when you get to the door," Brandon says with an awkward look at me.

"I can't wait to get on the boat," the second girl sounds excited. "Gold Rush is going to be lit. Make sure you save some wuk-ups for me." She reaches over and squeezes his arm as if she is unable to resist touching him. I don't blame her because his muscles are popping under that polo shirt.

"Let me catch up with you guys later," Brandon looks uncomfortable. "Faye and I were talking ..."

At the mention of my name the two girls finally acknowledge my presence, as if Brandon's words had conjured me up out of the air.

"No, that's fine," I jam the cover on my lunch container shut. "I have a lot of work to finish so I'll just leave you guys to your conversation."

I jump to my feet and walk away, ignoring Brandon's protests.

I feel stupid for thinking that he was asking me out on a date while it is now clear to me that he just wanted to hang out as friends. For a while there I let myself forget that he is Mr. Popular, Mr. Party Organiser, Mr. Ladies' Man. Not once in all our conversations has he mentioned this Gold Rush cruise that is obviously going on tonight. No doubt all the Instagram girls will soon have pictures up on their feeds, looking glamorous in their skimpy outfits. I bite my lip as I walk out of the lunchroom, not even sure why I feel so upset and stupid. Stupid, stupid, stupid.

When Saturday evening rolls around I'm still in a bad mood. I spent the morning supermarket shopping, cleaning the house and doing laundry. I keep myself busy so that I don't sit around the house and brood over the loss of something that never really was. Brandon messaged me from the moment I got back to my desk, apologizing for the interruption at lunch and saying that he still wanted to see the movie if I was free. I lie and tell him that I have a date that night but maybe some other time. That's a nice vague answer which is sure to let him know that he is not a priority in my life. He seems to get the message loud and clear because his response is curt: Sure, np...And that is the last I have heard from him.

I decide to get a shower and change my clothes then drop off the stuff I got at the supermarket for Nicky and the girls. I usually buy some fruit and healthy snacks to last them throughout the week, as well as a few treats. Stuff that my mother's salary alone can't cover, and Alicia can't buy since she never keeps a job. I pull up my favourite playlist on my phone and turn up the volume, singing along in the shower and letting the warm water wash over me. I feel strangely upbeat when I get out and I decide to dress in something nice then take myself out for something to eat after I leave my mother's house. I even take extra care with my makeup, applying a soft gold glittery eyeshadow and a pretty peach lipgloss. I lightly spritz my thick long braids with some oil sheen and I am good to go.

When I reach my mother's house, I notice that the car isn't there. I have a cute second-hand car but since I'm driving Aunt Niya's jeep while she is away, my mother has full use of my car. I knock on the kitchen door, and hearing no response, let myself in with my key. I place the grocery bags on the table and start unpacking. I will put away everything and message my mother or Dante to let them know.

"Faye," my father enters the room so quietly that it startles me.

I spin around. "I didn't realize anyone was here," I say.

"The others went to get pizza," he says. "I was in the back working on a painting for a show that's coming up."

My father is an artist. When I used to watch him paint he would make the canvas come to life with bold swipes of his knife or his brush before stepping back to observe his work with a critical eye. He is good. The kind of 'selling your art in a gallery' good. Once when I was about ten or so he took me to an art show and pointed to some paintings he had done which were hanging on the wall. I felt fussy holding his hand while these well dressed, rich people came up telling him how wonderful his work was.

"Okay," I take the fruit out of the shopping bag and go to place it in the fridge.

"You don't have to do that anymore," my father says.

"Do what?" I am confused.

"Bring stuff for Nicky and the girls, lend Alicia money, take care of everybody. You don't need to do it anymore. Like I told you, I'm back and I'm going to be a better father. Your mother and I will handle the bills."

"Back until you decide you're leaving again," I laugh sarcastically.

"I'm not going anywhere," my father is firm. "You've helped take care of everybody; you did stuff I should have been doing but wasn't able to. That was a lot of pressure to put on a young girl. I want you to take care of Faye now. "In fact," he pauses. "I want to help you take care of Faye. If you ever need anything, I want you to know that you can always call me."

I know that my family loves me, but no-one apart from Aunt Niya has told me that they want to help take care of me. I help take care of them, that's the way it is, and although I never had a problem doing it, the thought of it working in reverse almost makes me cry. Then I remember who it is talking. My father creates art out of a blank canvas and hope out of words. The art I can trust. It is real and tangible; I can run my fingers over it. The words I can't trust. They fall into the air, disappear and you later wonder if you imagined them.

I put the biscuits away in silence.

"I could never take care of you all the way I wanted to because I couldn't even take care of myself." He has my attention. I look up.

"I was an alcoholic. When you and Alicia were little I just used to drink at weekends then sober up, but by the time Dante and then Nicky came along I was drunk most of the time. I would give your mother money to help in the house and spend the rest of it in a rum shop or a bar. Your mother wouldn't let me come around you all like that so after a while I would go sober up, cry, beg, promise her that things would be different and then do it all over again. Sometimes I would be good for months but the alcohol just kept calling me and no matter how I tried I couldn't resist."

"Are you still drinking?" I ask with my hands folded across my chest. I think of Nicky and the girls and how crushed they will be when he leaves. What is my mother thinking? Is she even thinking?

"I haven't had a drink in four years. I'm committed to not drinking again. I went to Verdun House and got help. I talk to my old counsellor almost every day."

I nod like it all makes sense, and in a way it does. It explains the coming and going and the long periods when we wouldn't see him.

"After your mother put me out, I never thought that we would get back together or that I would get the chance to be close to my children," he says. "We never lost contact and a couple years ago I let her know I wasn't drinking anymore but it took a long time to convince her that I could stay sober."

I nod again. I didn't even know that my mother had put him out. I didn't even know she had it in her. I have a lot of questions, but I don't know where to begin and I still don't know if I can trust my father. I don't even want to look at him and his Dante/Nicky eyes in case I begin to believe him and hope again. In the silence that falls between us my eyes flit around the room, eventually landing on him despite my best efforts.

"You're even more beautiful than when I saw you years ago," he says. "You always had the prettiest skin and a smile that would light up a room."

My eyes feel wet. He thinks I am beautiful. Not pretty for a dark-skinned girl or pretty for a fat girl. He doesn't use the qualifying words that I never understand; the words that imply that dark-skinned girls or fat girls aren't expected to be pretty. Does anyone ever say pretty for a clear-skinned girl or a slim girl? And he thinks I have the prettiest skin, the same skin some Bajan men have a problem with. I am the darkest one in my family. I have my grandmother's complexion while everyone else has my father and mother's medium brown skin tone. I blink and bite down on my lip. I'm not going to let him get to me.

We hear the slamming of car doors and then my mother, Nicky, the girls and Dante are in the house. Nicky and the girls are talking excitedly and Dante is carrying two boxes of pizza. I almost don't recognize my mother. She is wearing a pair of capri jeans and a pink blouse. Her short natural hair looks like it has been freshly twisted. She is wearing nail polish – a nice nude colour - and lip gloss! Nicky, Jalia and Jalicia crowd around my father. The only person missing is Alicia, and, just as I think of her, she comes through the door.

"I hope y'all left some pizza for me," she says.

"We're now about to eat," my father says. "How did everything go at work?"

Alicia has a job?

"I'm the receptionist at a spa." Alicia proudly answers my unspoken question. "I just started yesterday. I was going to tell you...It's not an office job like yours, and it obviously doesn't pay as much as yours, but I like it."

"That's fantastic," I say, and I mean it. An office job would never suit a free spirit like Alicia. "You'll do great interacting with the clients and organizing appointments."

"Thanks," she smiles, looking pleased.

Nicky and the girls are already seated at the table, pointing out which slices of pizza they want from the two open boxes. My mother is placing plates and glasses on the table. Alicia rushes over to help her. My father squeezes Dante on the shoulder and smiles at something my brother says to him. He looks at Dante then looks around the room with clear, focused eyes and his smile widens. In that smile I can actually feel the love he has for everyone. I can't stop looking at him, at them. He must feel my eyes on him, and his smile doesn't waver as he looks my way.

"Why don't you stay and eat with us? There's more than enough for everybody," my father says.

"Yes, stay," my mother echoes.

"Daddy, I'm starving," Nicky calls from the table.

I feel a mixture of emotions. Happy, sad, scared, confused, hopeful. I'm starving too, for my Daddy's love. I feel overwhelmed like I need to run far away although I really want to stay. My mother looks disappointed when I don't reply. My father stands behind her and rubs his hands up and down her arms before dropping a brief kiss on her temple.

An image of Sean and Stacy flashes across my mind. Every. Single. Morning. They. Kiss.

My family life isn't pretty like Sean and Stacy's; in fact, it's messy and pretty complicated, but away from my gaze my family has been building what I have been craving from the time I was a child, and what I still crave when I watch Sean and Stacy every morning. In a flash I realize that all that's gold doesn't glitter; sometimes it's tarnished and needs to be polished over time. I need time to process this so I let a lie slip off my tongue easily.

"I'm on my way to meet someone for dinner. Maybe some other time." When I say 'some other time' I actually mean it.

"Oh," my mother's face brightens. "You have a date. I was saying to myself that you looked extra special."

"Come to lunch tomorrow," my father says.

I agree and rush out the door before the tears start rolling down my face.

I drive to Limegrove. Aunt Niya lives in St. James and it will be a short drive back home. I wander around a bit looking in the store windows, then I decide to see if the cinema has any tickets left for the movie I was going to see with Brandon. I'm in luck, so I pay for my ticket and order my food. I hear my name and turn around.

It's Brandon, and he looks good even though he is just wearing a blue t-shirt and jeans.

"You could have just told me you were coming to see the movie with someone else," he says dully.

"I'm not on a date. That fell through." Lying is coming too easily to me today but I don't want to admit that I never had a date in the first place.

"You're beautiful." He is looking me up and down. "Only an idiot would miss a date with you."

I laugh. I feel my mood start to lighten. I am beautiful. I always knew it, but it feels good to hear my father and Brandon say it.

"So, are you and this guy who's not here serious?" Brandon asks.

"No, I don't even know him, really." I swear this is my last lie for the night.

"So it's no problem if I get a seat next to yours and we make this our first date? You know I like you, right?"

"I wasn't sure," I reply with a little grin.

It turns out that Brandon didn't ask me to go to the cruise because he didn't think it was the right place to have our first date since he would be working all night. I don't know where this will go, like I don't know how things with my father will go. But I'm tired of being guarded and not living my life. Brandon grabs my hand as we walk into the cinema. I feel young and carefree. It's a strange but welcome feeling and I try not to let my smile split my face.

CHAPTER EIGHT

Mhizz Iz V.2.0/Step Up in Life/Vibrate Higher

When a man want to beg back he does do all kinda foolishness like calling yuh phone all de time and messaging yuh 24-7. So I din surprised when I see a instant message from Darius Monduh night. We did fall out the night before and he play he ain talk to me fuh de whole a Monduh but dah did a bare joke cause yuh done know I din' talking back to he first. I know he did soon gine come crawling back once he come to he senses anyway. He send de message at 7:08 p.m. and I read um widdout opening it so he wouldn't see nuh blue ticks if he did checking.

Darius: I need to talk to you.

I look at dah and look off and went back watching makeup videos online. Yuh cahn reply to men as soon as duh message yuh 'cause dem would think yuh ain doing nuttin' but drawing up 'bout de place waiting pon dem. When I look back at de phone it was 9:18 pm and I see I had another message and two missed phone calls but I left he ass pon read. I doze off fuh a lil bit and at 11:23p.m. de phone buzzing wake me up and it did he again wid a next message. Why he doan try and sleep or sain? I shut off de phone and roll over in de bed cause I would gaw deal wid he in de morning.

When I wake up Tuesduh I turn on de phone and check my messages as usual. The first thing I does reach fuh pon a morning is de phone. Is actually sleep next to me in de bed cause sometimes I does fall sleep messaging Darius or Kaneisha or looking at tings pun Instagram or TikTok or sain. Anyhow, I finally read de rest of de messages:

Darius: Iz, you can't answer the phone? 7:11 P.M.

Darius: You could stop pretending to ignore me. 7:13 P.M.

Darius: Iz, call me. 9:18 P.M.

Darius: Seriously? This is how you moving? I know you ain sleeping yet. 11:23 P.M.

Darius: I going to sleep. You is something else. 12:02 AM

He leh a whole blasted day pass and den want to be blowing up my phone last night? It don't work so. Anyhow, I decide to message he back.

Izcara: Was busy and ain get to check my phone 'til just now. 5:46 A.M.

Darius: "Calling you now."   5:46 A.M.

Before I finish reading, de phone start ringing in my hand.

"Yeah," I did still vex wid he so I ain call he bae or babe or nuttin so. Anyhow, yuh gotta let men mek back up wid you first, so I did waiting 'pon he to apologize.

"Yeah Iz. Sorry I couldn't call you yesterday, but you know I had training all day."

I did fahget bout dah, to tell de trute. He always got some kinda training at work but I sure he coulda find time to call me during de break or when he went to the bathroom or sain. I ain say nuttin so he went long talking.

"I was thinking about what happened between us all yesterday. It had me so offset I couldn't concentrate on training."

Even though he couldn't see me I did smiling. Darius voice real sexy, especially early in de morning. I din really sleep dah good last night neider. I keep waking up and missing Darius then dropping back to sleep. It seem like he did missing me too. I did still vex bout wuh he say bout my hair and ghetto behavior but I guess I coulda listen to he first before I start quarrelling bout Rochelle. So even though I din gine tell he so, I was glad that he call to apologize. Darius is the first body I did really like since Tre.

"I was trying to get you all last night," Darius did sound frustrated.

"Sorry, I was busy then I went sleep early."

"Anyway, I was thinking a lot about us...and I realize that this just isn't going to work out. I have to concentrate on work and my exams and is too much drama with you all the time. I wanted things to work out but I need something different."

I was in summuch shock I almost couldn't begin to talk. But once I open my mouth de words start jumping out.

"Something different or somebody different? Like Rochelle Grant?"

"See what I mean? You know I don't move like that. I done tell you me and Rochelle are just friends. Sunday you couldn't talk like an adult. You had to leave one time. All last night you pretend not to see my messages or get my phone calls. I can't deal with this type of behavior."

"Right. I fahget I too ghetto fabulous for you."

Darius laugh but not a 'ha ha ha' laugh. "Look, I got some clothes and things you left here. When I could drop them off?"

Just so de man dun wid me and it din even six o'clock in the morning yet. WTF JUST HAPPEN?

"Izzie, you ask fuh dat."

Imagine Trina had de gall to tell me dat. Like somebody ask she fuh advice. I was putting back in she weave and telling she bout how me and Darius brek up and dah is wuh she gine tell me. Trina is my cousin. She fadduh and my fadduh is brudduhs.

"How you mean?"

"Well," Trina screw up she face. "First, you had no right messaging he so early in the morning. He would got to wait til evening to hear me. Next thing, you let Darius mess wid you head. When you find out bout another woman de worst thing you could do is keep noise and get up in a man face. Yuh is to give dem a taste a dem own medicine. Why you din't find some man face to skin up in and put it pon IG fuh he to see? Men could give but they can't tek."

"Darius don't really be pon IG."

"Wuh dah got to do wid anything? He got friends or know people that would see it and tell he. You really got to learn how to handle men, Izzie."

I guess Trina feel she is the only body that know 'bout men. Just because she got a man that does pay she rent and give she money. She man is an Indian. Not Indian from India though. One that born in Barbados and he got nuff money. And a wife. But that doan bother Trina and I guess it doan bother he neither.

"Anyhow, you need to stop wasting time wid men like Darius and find a man that could do something fuh you. I keep telling you that I could introduce you to some proper men."

"I could find men myself."

"Yeah, but what type?" Trina wrinkle up she nose like she smell something bad. "Darius is a nice fellow and he got potential but you ain got time to waste pon potential. I could introduce you to men who got money now."

"You better try and work fuh you own money."

"Wuh you think I is be doing with Rajkumar?"

All I could do is laugh cause Trina head ain good. I tell she so to she face nuff times but she is a big able woman so she could do whatever she feel like. De ting is Trina could leff dah sorta behavior fuh women dat cahn do nuh better. She got a good job at a bank and she got de type of looks men like. Pretty with light brown skin and when she got in she fourteen-inch weave you would swear is she own hair. I does wear weave when I feel like but Trina gotta wear weave 'cause she like men to feel she got long hair. I wonder if Rajkumar does feel all the tracks in she head? Or if one ever pop off in he hand?

Anyway, we was downstairs in de living room in she townhouse watching a movie while I was putting in she weave. Trina live in a one-bedroom townhouse in CircleSquare. Yes, dat CircleSquare, de gated community wha' part people wid money does live. Or people like Trina dat got people wid money. Darius apartment nice but not like this.

"Three more girls at the bank want you to do weave fuh dem," Trina tell me.

One thing bout Trina, she does be good at getting business fuh me. When she step out she does look flawless and everybody does want tuh know who do she hair.

"Anyway, I was thinking bout something," she say. "Is time fuh you to upgrade youself and step up in life. You don't get tired butting bout de place going at people house doing hair? Is time you try and get a salon or something, Iz."

"I was thinking de same thing. Zay want me work wid she in de salon."

Trina let out a big able stupse. "Nuhbody ain talking bout working in the back of Swan Street with Zay. You need to attract a certain clientele but not the sort that gine want to be up and down town. I was thinking maybe somewhere pon de South Coast. I feel we should rent a space. You could do hair and makeup and I could sell clothes and accessories."

Trina is a hustler. She does hustle de men at de bank, she does hustle Rajkumar and she does sell clothes and earrings and handbags and dah sorta ting. She dun tell me dat when she and Rajkumar break up she is to got money pon de bank, not like some a dem foolish girls who does got men who does handle money and does only buy nuff clothes and pose wid red bottom shoes den when duh get stran out all duh got is de clothes hanging up in a wardrobe. Not a proper car, not a house or piece a land. Trina got good taste in clothes. Is just dat everything she wear does be a size too small. She always gine way so she does buy tings to bring back and sell. Trina too slack but she does bring back tings and give me and Trequon. But den I doan charge she fuh putting in de big lotta weave she always wearing so fair is fair.

"So wuh you think?" Trina ask.

I did still thinking. I ain sure if I want to be in nuh business wid Trina. Is true dat she would bring good clients but I feel me and she would get way. Plus Zay is my girl and it would look bad if I went and open a shop wid Trina when Zay did asking me all de time to work wid she.

"I gaw think bout dah lil mo," I tell Trina.

"I serious Iz," she say. "So think 'bout it and I gine start looking to see where we could rent."

I ain say nuttin so she seem to think dat dah mean de answer is yes. Dah is classic Trina. Real bossy and own way.

"How much longer this gine tek? I got to go to the opening of a new lounge at seven o'clock".

"Relax, Trina. Is only four o'clock right now and I gine be done in anudder twenty minutes or so."

"Good. Why you don't come wid me? The invitation is for me and a guest. I would drop you back home afterwards. Is better than you stopping home fretting 'bout Darius or worse, picking up the phone to call he."

"Nah, dah is too much stress. I would gaw guh home and dress and dah gine be too rushing now."

"You could bathe and dress from here. I sure I got something here that would fit you. And we does wear the same shoe size," Trina start getting excited fuh de company. I forget that she doan get to guh nuhwhere so with Rajkumar cause somebody that know he or he wife might be dey. Dah ain really mek nuh sense to me tho cause he always at she townhouse and Barbados small so it ain like he could hide.

To tell de truth, gine out wid Trina might be cool. It was Saturday so Trequon did spending de night by he fadduh and I ain really had nuttin else to do.

"I guess I could go." I say.

Dah lounge party did sain else. Duh had bare bougie people up in dey. De same ones yuh does see pon IG posing at certain restaurants or pon vacation in Rome, Prague and Paris wid hashtags like #EuropeanVacay #dolcevita #LondonNights

Trina ain pon dem level. De furthest place she does get wid Rajkumar is Miami. Anyhow, she like she know a lot of dem cause when we walk thru de reception every five seconds somebody did waving at she or stopping and kissing she pon she cheek. As usual de had more women than men and all de women did looking at one annuduh to see who makeup did de most and who did dress de best. A group of bout eight old women did running all 'bout de lounge wid a selfie stick tekking pictures wid dem hand pon dem hip and mekking duck lips. Look, when people reach thirty-five and forty and up in dem sorta numbers duh could really stop home and dun wid dis big lotta gine bout at parties posing. It does look foolish.

Anyhow, I did dey talking wid Trina when who walk in but Rajkumar and anudder man. Trina really bring me hay so she and she man could be together? I look at she stink and she play she rolling she eyes at me. Before I could turn round good Rajkumar and de man did up unneat we.

"Izzie, dis is my friend Omar. Omar, dis is Trina cousin Izcara." You cahn talk more Bajan than Rajkumar.

"This is the Izzie that you were telling me about?" Omar ask Trina.

"Yeah."

"Pleased to meet you Izzie," Omar squeeze me hand.

He start wrong. First of all, he just meet me so I ain know why he calling me Izzie. Next thing, I ain know he like dah so why he all up in my face skinning he teet and squeezing my hand?

"You're even more beautiful than the picture Trina sent me." Dis Omar man was doing the most. I know I did look good in a short leopard print spaghetti strap dress and a pair a red shoes dat did burning my foot, but he did really getting on extra.

Wait, wuh he mean by de picture Trina send he? I tell he 'excuse me' and pull Trina one side.

"Why you send he my picture?"

"I told him you were coming and I wanted him to meet you. He did want to see wuh you look like. Omar loaded, girl. I done tell you to stop dealing wid men wid potential and deal wid men dat got something already."

"I dun tell you I don't move so."

Trina screw up she face. "Whatever. But don't get on like a idiot now. He's Rajkumar good friend and I don't feel like hearing bout how you carry he long scruffy."

She flounce back over to Rajkumar and left me to talk to Omar. I shoulda never come nowhere wid she. I don't like common class behaviour and Trina really getting on like she want me to pimp myself out.

Twenty minutes later and I did still trying to get rid a Omar. No matter wuh I do or where I turn de man did stick on pon me like glue. I din even responding to de talk he did running but he tell me how one he like a challenge and he gine break me down. Then he ask me out to Nikki Beach like gine to Nikki Beach could mek me tolerate he.

Anyhow, he snatch up my hand and start telling me he like me and if we could leff in hay and go for a drink. He did thirsty fuh real but he mussee think I is a real idiot. Yuh does leff somewhere wid a man you ain even know? He mussee see de look pon my face cause then he say Raj and Trina could come long if I frighten to be alone wid he.

Stupse.

Just as I did trying to pull way my hand, who walk in but Darius and one Rochelle Grant? I ain gaw lie. I did so shocked that I even fahget bout Omar holding my hand and just stare at the two a dem. Looka dis fuckery hay so. Dem walk bout talking to people and skinning dem teet then Darius look round and spot me and step way from Rochelle quick so. Next thing I know he did next to me and Omar telling me he want to talk to me fuh a minute. I roll my eyes but I did want to hear what he could possibly say to explain why he in dey wid Rochelle, so I yank my hand way from Omar and went to talk to Darius.

"So this is what you doing now Izzie? You moving like Trina?"

"Wuh business a yours it is wuh I do? You ain de same body dat brek up wid me this morning?"

"I never thought you would turn out to be a ho like your cousin. So you're into married men with money too?"

When he say dat I did feel like somebody cuff me in my stomach. If de got two men in the world I would never expect to hear something like that from it would be Tre and Darius. I couldn't even hide the water in my eyes when I look at he. I gine kill Trina fuh trying to hook me up wid a married man but dah gine got to wait til later.

"Trina just introduced me to him. I don't know nothing bout him and I ain interested. But you should know me better than that."

Darius turn red.

"Iz, sorry. I know you're not like that. Just seeing you with him made the blood rush to my head."

"But why? You finished with me and I see your friend Rochelle here with you. So why you care who you see me with?"

"Forget Rochelle. I keep telling you we're not in anything. I think you and I need to talk and see if we can work things out."

"Work things out with a man who could call me a ho? You got me confused wid somebody else."

Thank God I did push my purse in the handbag I borrow from Trina to carry to the cocktail reception. I had enough money to get a taxi home and if I ain had enough I would beg Kaneisha or Chanelle to come and pick me up. Dis is de last time I gine cry over Darius ass. I walk out de cocktail party without looking back at he, Trina, Rajkumar or Omar. In she own way Trina right though she does go bout things de wrong way. Is time fuh me to do something different cause Lord knows wuh I doing ain't working fuh me.

CHAPTER NINE

Elwood A. B. Jones, Kayode and the Twistory Lesson

It was hot. Blazing hot. Every so often a little breeze wafted through the air, lightly kissing the skin before quickly retreating. It was hard to remember that it was only March and that sometimes the nights were still cool, almost as cool as the days were hot.

It was in this heat that Kayode, the artist formerly known as Joseph Cumberbatch, walked dispiritedly from house to house in CircleSquare, trying to sell his books. It was early Saturday morning, barely past 8 o'clock. Most of the residents of CircleSquare were at home except for the weekend warriors like Bree Highland who at that very moment was midway through her first round of sun salutations in yoga class. Or Ryan Nicholls who was deadlifting in the gym. Or Susan, Lynn and Ron who were jogging along the pristine streets and avenues of CircleSquare. In many houses, children sullenly dressed for a morning of lessons in preparation for the Eleven Plus or CAPE exams. Others gathered up their supplies for various lessons: swimming, dancing, music, tennis and cricket. There was hardly a child in CircleSquare with free time on a Saturday morning. Saturday morning was as bad as a weekday morning except that you didn't wear a school uniform, the children often grumbled to each other. The parents of school-aged children readied themselves for a day of ferrying their offspring to and from the stops on their packed itineraries (The mothers exclaimed to each other as they dropped off and picked up their children: "I'm a glorified taxi driver!" or "I never get a minute to myself!").

That Saturday morning John Peters defiantly cranked up his lawnmower, not caring about the email he would surely receive in short order from Elwood Jones about disturbing the peace and quiet of the neighbourhood. John was violating the unwritten rule that no lawn mowers be used in CircleSquare before 9 o'clock on a weekend morning. The problem with Elwood Jones, John thought darkly, was that he thought he knew more law than actual lawyers. That was typical nowadays, especially with so many graduates of the University of Google Law School. The lawnmower jerked forward, pulling John in its wake. He didn't really know what he was doing. He hardly mowed his own lawn; he was much too busy for that. However, that very morning it had been announced in the papers that he was being appointed as a Judge in the Supreme Court. He suddenly had the urge to get outside and experience the fresh air and sunshine. And to look learned and distinguished and humbly receive the congratulations his neighbours would undoubtedly shower upon him.

As John mowed the strip of lawn outside his gate, Kayode was being met with a reception generally only meted out to Jehovah's Witnesses or Seven Days' Adventists. He never made it past any of the electronic gates. The owners didn't bother to open them when the security cameras showed who was outside. At houses where people deigned to look out, a few politely indicated that they were busy and suggested that he return at some other time. Implicit was the not-so-subtle suggestion that they were not interested and would prefer that he never returned. Several people were outside picking up the newspapers or puttering around. The majority of them bypassed subtlety altogether and simply said a point blank "no" without even engaging him in conversation.

It was disheartening but not surprising. Kayode didn't expect the residents of CircleSquare, with their upper middle-class insulation from the life of the average Bajan, to identify with Pan African/Caribbean writings such as his. Admittedly his books weren't best sellers even among his crowd. In fact, they weren't sellers at all, but everyone knew that the life of an artist was hard and that Bajans never supported their own. Even (Black) Jesus himself had said that a prophet is not without honour except in his own town, among his own relatives and in his own home. Kayode was certainly without honour in all of the above, but he would keep on trodding.

It was sooooo embarrassing, Lanisha Cumberbatch thought as she looked down from behind the safety of her bedroom window curtain at her father walking from door to door throughout the neighbourhood.

It was like he was trying to kill her with shame.

Didn't he know that some of the children she went to school with lived on this street? Graison Peirce lived a few doors down. Kai Stuart lived at the end of the street. And horror of horrors, Rachel Brathwaite and her brothers Devin and Dean lived one avenue away. Rachel, one of the most popular girls in school. Dean, the straight A student with the innocent smile who everyone knew was far from innocent. And there was Devin, the future famous rock guitarist who Lanisha had a secret crush on for the longest time. Lanisha crossed her fingers and prayed to baby Jesus, the white one with blond hair who she prayed to in times of crises like this, that her father would give up and get tired before he got anywhere near to the Brathwaites' house. For insurance, she threw in a prayer to adult Jesus, the one in the flowing robes with the long blond hair and Jesus sandals. She would die – just curl up in a ball and die – if her father tried to sell his books to anyone who went to school with her. Like literally.

She walked away from the window and paced up and down anxiously. Maybe no one would realize that he was her father. After all, they had only been living here for about six weeks or so. It wasn't that long ago that Uncle David, her father's brother, had reluctantly asked her father to house-sit for him while he was overseas studying for a year. Lanisha looked at herself in the mirror, her dark skin smooth and unblemished, thick natural hair in a large Afro puff. She took after her mother. Her father was brown-skinned with brown eyes, dark brown dreadlocks and a thick, bushy beard. There was probably no way that the average person could tell that he was her father. No, there was definitely no way. She looked well put together and normal while her father looked like, well, she didn't want to be the one to say it, but he looked like ...

A bearded fig tree.

The man looked like a human bearded fig tree, Elwood Jones thought as he laid eyes on the unkempt being who introduced himself as Kayode. Had Pedro a Campos, the Portuguese explorer who named Barbados "Los Barbados" (presumably after the island's bearded fig trees) laid eyes on Kayode, he might have mistaken him for a bearded fig tree. Someone needed to take a weed whacker to Kayode and trim all that bush on his person.

Elwood Jones spoke to Kayode for a few minutes then returned to his porch where he had been reading before the man turned up selling his 'Back to Africa' books. Nonsense. Had anyone in Africa told these people they wanted them to come back? And what would they do in Africa, having achieved their life-long goal of going back there? Return to the Caribbean?

As Elwood Jones sat down and unfolded the newspaper, his knobby knees shot out from the khaki knee-length shorts he favoured. He was all long limbs and spectacles. He looked like one of the history books or literary tomes he liked to read; dry and somewhat withered, the lines under his eyes and the parentheses around his mouth as permanent as a crease in a dog-eared corner of a page.

Troy Layne and Elaine observed him from Elaine's driveway across the street.

"He looks like he used to wear a pocket protector in school," Troy announced. "Like he would always be carrying fountain pens that would leak."

"He reminds me of something," Elaine said. "You know, one of those insects you used to see once upon a time? The long bony one that you hardly see nowadays. I can't remember what you call them, but he reminds me of one of them. He looks like..."

"A god horse?" Troy asked.

"Yes!" Elaine snorted with laughter. He looks just like a god horse."

The god horse and the human bearded fig tree made for a very curious sight as they patrolled the neighbourhood two evenings later.

"I guess Elwood A.B Jones, Esquire found a way to nag Coyote into doing the neighbourhood watch with him," Kristin Yarde said as she stood behind a curtain peeping at the two men walking past her house.

"Who's Coyote?" Her husband asked without looking away from the latest breaking news on CNN.

"The man that came around selling books."

"You mean Kayode?" Her husband laughed. "You bought one of his books and still don't even know the man's name?"

"I only bought it because I felt sorry for him," Kristin said. "And I feel sorrier now because he's stuck with Elwood Jones."

"So, you're not going to read the book? You love reading. Your nose is always in your Kindle."

Kristin shot her husband a withering look. "I don't like local authors. Always writing some fake deep 'literary' crap." She made air quotation marks. "Boring. Then they act surprised that no one buys their books. People want books they can relax and enjoy. Like *Fifty Shades of Grey* or even Danielle Steele or Nora Roberts. Why can't they write books like that?"

It was a valid question.

In one of the more modest (by CircleSquare standards) homes at the end of the street, Lanisha fretted as she sat at the dining room table with her mother Nicole and brother Dwaine. Not only was the house modest, but there wasn't a new or higher-end vehicle in the garage. Her uncle's seven-year-old jeep was parked next to her father's almost fifteen-year-old Suzuki Baleno, which ran due to a combination of luck and divine intervention.

"Why is he doing this?" She dragged out the last two words in the sentence. "I am like literally at a loss as to why he's doing this."

"You mean doing the neighbourhood watch with that weirdo?" Dwaine asked.

"Yeah, but why is he doing any of this? Like, why did he just wake up one day and decide that he didn't want to be Joseph Cumberbatch, but he wanted to be Kayode? Why did he start dressing in African shirts and sandals instead of normal clothes? Why did he become 'conscious'?"

"I don't know, Lanisha." Her mother said tiredly. That wasn't strictly true. It was more accurate to say that she didn't understand. It had started out innocently enough, with Joseph reading an article in the newspaper about the need for Britain to pay reparations for slavery in the West Indies. Soon he fell down the rabbit hole of internet research and started talking about The Case for Reparations/Britain's Black Debt/How Europe Underdeveloped Africa. He clicked link after link, reliving the atrocities of slavery and complaining bitterly about the historical injustices of the past and how certain people in Barbados had been given a head start that others could never catch up to. Then he got obsessed with the Windrush generation and how it wasn't enough that Britain had profited from slavery, it still wanted to profit more from the labour of black people doing jobs white people didn't want to do. Nicole wasn't unduly concerned at this stage. Joseph had a way of becoming enthused about things, throwing all his energy into them, and then almost as abruptly, losing interest altogether. It was only after he attended a lecture on reparations that she felt the first pin pricks of worry. The little seed of aggravation that the newspaper article planted in him started to take root and flourish. He cast off "European attire" for Afrocentric garb: Ankara print, kente cloth and dashikis. His hair was the next thing to change. The little rolled up knots he sported while growing his hair into locks had irritated her no end. Then there was the day he announced that he would no longer be using his slave name but now wished to be referred to as Kayode.

"Kayode?" She had repeated the name blankly.

"Yes, Kayode," he said proudly. "The Yoruba were one of the main groups of slaves brought into Barbados as you should know. Kayode is Yoruba for "he brought joy".

"Is that so?" she asked with a dour expression on her face.

The entire thing was ridiculous. Britain wasn't going to pay anyone reparations. They would continue to be in the red for their black debt. The Bajan descendants of slave masters had a financial head start of a few hundred years but how did complaining about that help her pay her bills? Europe may have underdeveloped Africa yet based on the African films she watched, some African people were doing very well. The people in those films drove luxury cars, lived in mansions and wore designer clothes. Was she to lose sleep over people who were living better than she was? And what was she to tell her family and friends who wanted to know if Joseph was going off? How would she explain this "slave name" foolishness?

"Joseph," she tried to appeal to whatever common sense he still possessed. "I really think that..."

"Kayode," he had reminded her. "My name is Kayode."

Unaware of the stir they were creating in the neighbourhood, the god horse and the human bearded fig tree struck up a forced conversation as they walked along.

"So Kayode, what do you do for a living?" Elwood Jones asked. He had no real interest in Kayode's occupation. He had no desire to talk to the man at all, but someone needed to take the neighbourhood watch patrols seriously and Kayode was the first person who had agreed to join him. "Agreed" was a strong word, Elwood Jones conceded silently. He had more or less bribed the man, buying a copy of each of the two books he had written, then when Kayode's eyes had glazed over with gratitude, asked him if he would be so kind as to help him kick off the neighbourhood watch patrol. Forty dollars was a small price to pay for getting Kayode to agree. Barbados wasn't as safe as it used to be. Maybe the residents of CircleSquare would be shamed into participation once they saw the two of them making the rounds.

"I work in the Ministry of Agriculture," Kayode said. "With greenhouses."

"Really?" Elwood Jones' interest was piqued. He loved plants. "Doing what exactly?"

They carried on an actual conversation for several minutes. When it petered out, the uncomfortable silence of two people who had little in common fell between them as they each racked their brains for what to talk about next. Mentally exhausted, Kayode asked, "What do you do?"

"I recently retired but I lectured history at the University for many years. And I wrote two books on Caribbean history," Elwood Jones said proudly.

"So, you're one of those twistorians who corrupt young people's minds?"

"Pardon me?"

"You know, selling people a version of history you want them to believe. Telling the youth lies about Christopher Columbus discovering the New World. New to who? Just because he didn't know about it? How do you discover some place that was there all the time with people already living on it?"

"I don't..." Elwood Jones started to protest but Kayode continued as if he hadn't spoken.

"Christopher Columbus was lost. He didn't know where the hell he was. He called people Indians because he thought he had landed in the Indies. He befriended the natives then killed them off. A typical coloniser and people like you try to entrench Babylon system by teaching people's children a big bundle of lies."

"You have no idea what I taught," Elwood Jones said sternly. He was well aware of the true story of Christopher Columbus and his penchant for renaming lands which already had a name.

"I know what they teach in school and the university. And I know how you people operate. People in CircleSquare don't care about black history and reparations as long as y'all driving your Mercedes and BMW. I bet for all the history you taught you never went on a single Emancipation Day Walk. But you would go and listen to classical music in Frank Collymore Hall or something so."

Elwood Jones, who drove a carefully preserved Mercedes, and was a great fan of classical music, reflected on the stupidity of Kayode's argument. Of course he had never been on an Emancipation Day Walk. One didn't need to traipse around in the sun behind a bunch of people playing drums and dressed in African print and hand-made sandals to have an appreciation of the significance of the day.

"I think you will find that the overwhelming majority of Bajans, regardless of their social class, have never been on an Emancipation Day Walk," he huffed, partly in indignation and partly because he and Kayode were climbing up a slight incline approaching the roundabout by Sangria Avenue. Elwood Jones was in fairly good shape. He walked every day but at a more leisurely pace than the younger man was setting, and not while being involved in a heated conversation.

"True," said Kayode. "'Cause they don't appreciate the hardships our forefathers went through and the sacrifices that people like General Bussa made so we could be free. People think that when you talk about these things you're holding on to the past. Britain owes us, and they must pay but if we don't care about our history, how will they?"

"Fair enough." Elwood Jones had had enough of Kayode's ramblings. Normally he was eager to talk about history but there was nothing to be gained from doing so with Kayode, who clearly lived in a village on the outskirts of reality. The man was strange, from the brightly patterned shirt and matching pants he wore to his car that should have been consigned to a scrap metal heap. Even his brother thought so. He had asked Elwood Jones to be patient with Kayode, saying that no one understood why he was "like this" nowadays. Elwood Jones had felt sorry for David, but one couldn't choose family. He knew Kayode's type – bitter at the world for its perceived injustices against the small black man; couldn't be bothered to spend time educating and bettering themselves and expected a free handout from society. Deciding to prove his theory he said, "Tell me a little about yourself. Where did you grow up, where did you go to school?"

"I was raised in St. Joseph. I grew up with my mother and grandmother. Spent a lot of time roaming in the countryside and learning about plants and bush medicine. I went to primary school in St. Joseph then to Harrison College. Had to get up real early on a morning to get into town for school."

"Oh, you went to Harrison College?" Elwood James was surprised. "So did I."

"The way my old man's face lit up when I passed for Harrison College you would have thought we won money," Kayode said.

"Indeed." Elwood Jones remembered the look of sheer pride that had flashed across his own father's face when he had passed for Harrison College. He could still see the moment clearly now. His father had reached out and hugged him, murmuring "My boy, my boy!". It had taken him by surprise. His father, tall, stern and patrician, dispensed affection the same way he dispensed medicine in his pharmacy. Exactly and never exceeding the required dosage. Not a drop of emotion was spilled or wasted. A cut on the knee? That merited some mercurochrome and an admonition to chin up. Coming first in class? A pat on the back or a brief rub on the head. Passing for Harrison College? Unbridled joy in the form of a heartfelt hug.

"So your father was around, then?" Elwood Jones asked. "You said that you were raised by your mother and grandmother."

"Oh, he was around," Kayode said, leaning his head to the side. "He didn't live with us, but he would visit almost every weekend. He used to work in town and sometimes David, our sister Jackie and I would meet him there on Saturdays after he finished work and he would drive us home. Then he and our mother would take us by the sea or we would stay home and play games. And he would visit us every other Sunday afternoon."

Elwood Jones tried to remember playing games with his father. Elias Jones had been the head of the household and a strict disciplinarian. A hard worker, he left home bright and early every day to open his pharmacy and returned home in time for dinner every night. After dinner, he remained seated at the table, waiting for Elwood and his brother Edward to show him their completed homework. On Sundays, the entire family would go to church then return home to eat lunch together. His father's parents joined them for lunch after church sometimes. His grandmother would mix a jug of coconut water and a red soft drink, a concoction that Elwood Jones hated. To this day the taste of coconut water brought back memories of sitting at the dinner table in his stiffly starched shirt and tie, taking care to use the proper utensils and etiquette or risk enduring a lecture from his parents and grandparents.

"Did you have to go to church every Sunday too?" Elwood Jones asked. Sundays in the Jones' household was the Lord's day, and it went without saying that everyone went to church unless seriously ill. The family took up an entire pew of the church at morning service. On Sunday nights before they went to bed there was half an hour of Bible study.

"My grandmother took us to church at times, but my mother wasn't really one for church except at Easter and Christmas. Even as a youth I didn't like all that white man religion although my consciousness wasn't developed yet."

"I see," Elwood Jones said. "So your father wasn't in the church?"

"Oh, he was a big church man. Went to church every Sunday, even on the Sundays when he would go out to make deliveries in the afternoon. He owned a little pharmacy called E.M.J's and he would bring medicine to some of the older people in the countryside who couldn't get into town to fill prescriptions."

Elwood Jones had been listening to Kayode with half an ear while trying to figure out what it was about the way he spoke that seemed so familiar. His ears pricked up at Kayode's last sentence.

"Your father owned E.M.J's?" he asked slowly.

"Yes, until it was sold about twenty years ago. Did you know it?"

Elwood Jones stopped walking and turned to face Kayode. Was this man playing some sort of joke on him? Of course he knew E.M.J's, it was the pharmacy his own father Elias Montgomery Jones had owned and operated until he sold it about twenty years ago. Was Kayode saying that Elias Jones was his father as well? Elwood looked at the much younger man whose high brown complexion was a couple shades darker than his own skin. Underneath the overgrowth of beard and bushy dreadlocks, there was a thin face with a pointed chin that he could now see was very much like that of his grandfather Elias Senior. How had he missed it? And that's why Kayode's manner of speaking had seemed so familiar. There was a certain measured cadence in his voice that reminded Elwood of his grandfather, although the old man's voice had been silent for a few decades now. Even the way he leaned his head to the side was reminiscent of the old man.

With growing horror, he took a few steps back from Kayode. This wasn't possible. He wondered if, instead of being a so-called perpetrator of twistory, he had been its victim. Had he been fed a carefully curated narrative of a hardworking father who was a dedicated family man and a bastion of the church? Was it possible that all that time his father had a much younger family stashed away in the countryside, far from where they lived near Belleville? He had heard about such things happening in Barbados. He had heard about people who found out about numerous brothers and sisters at their father's funeral. It was common in the old days, but he didn't come from that sort of family.

He remembered how his father would pack a little valise full of medicine and various items to deliver to people in the countryside once or twice a month. No matter how hard he and Edward begged to go along for the drive his father sternly replied that he was going to be working and needed no distractions. Was this story Kayode recounted possible? Were he, Kayode, David and Edward brothers? Did he have a sister named Jackie? Did Kayode and David know, and had they moved into CircleSquare to get reparations in the form of a share of the money Elias James had left to his sons years ago? There were more questions than answers and Elwood Jones dared not pose a single one to Kayode.

"E.M.J's?" he stammered, pulling a spotless white handkerchief from the pocket of his spray-starched khaki shorts and mopping the sweat from his face. "E.M.J's..." Mind racing, he furrowed his brow in mock concentration. "Sorry, can't say I've ever heard of it."

CHAPTER TEN

Mhizz Iz Over And Out

Dis is wuh gine on:

Me and Darius done. D-U-N done like rh. He play he calling me after I left de reception and messaging me talking 'bout he sorry. I had to block he number so he could get the real message.

I shoulda never tek he on when he come up to me skinning he teet' in BBQ Barn. From de time I see he wid tenders I shoulda know he fail cause everybody know WingDings is life. You could tell a lot 'bout people from certain tings dem does like: conkies dat got in raisins or dem dat doan got in; sodabix or eclipse biscuits; livers or gizzards, end piece or inside piece of cokenut bread; pine or red Ju-C; sugar cake or tambrin balls; WingDings or tenders. He like de outside piece of cokenut bread – error. Everybody know yuh does eat de inside piece wid a slice a cheese.

I ain speak to Trina since dah night neider. I guess I would speak back to she eventually cause blood thicker than water.

Next ting is Barbados does mek me sick. De only way yuh does get thru hay is if you went to a big-up school or you family big up. Dah's why I ain't vote fuh a boy in de elections. Walking bout talking bout dem gine create jobs. Create jobs, my ass and know dem ain gine do one ting fuh nobody but demself. Doan care wuh you try to do in Barbados dem does find a way to stop poor people from getting thru. Yuh guh way and buy two tings and dem want to dig up yuh suitcase like dem unmekking it and charge yuh fuh every shite while dem let bare big-up people sail thru wid four and five pieces a luggage and doan even pull one suitcase one side and ask dem to ope it in. From de time you dress a certain way or does talk a certain way Bajans does feel dem know wuh you bout. And doan talk bout when duh find out wuh part you live or went school. Stupse.

Trina right bout one thing.

Is time I Vibrate Higher.

I tired a people acting like I is a little picky girl that could only butt bout and do hair at people house.

My fadduh send a ticket fuh me to go to New York and tell me try and come up dey and do a hair or makeup course and he would help me open a shop when I get back home. Dat is time I settle and do something proper fuh myself and mek sure I got money and health insurance and tings like dah. At first I din sure wuh to do cause the last time I went up by he I had de most traumatizing experience of my young life and swear I din gine back.

Now I know New York full a freaks and yuh does got to be careful but I din expecting nuttin like wuh happen. I went up dey fuh a few days to get some hair supplies. De Saturday night did my fadduh wife Melanie birthday. Anyway, de two a dem dress up and went out to dinner at some expensive restaurant. My fadduh did dress in a black suit and Melanie had on a hi-lo red dress. Duh did look too sweet. I went in de bedroom and fall sleep watching TV. I was tired cause I did spend the day all bout de place buying hair dat people at home did want and a few tings I could hustle pun de side. One Kaneisha ask me to buy a black jumpsuit fuh she and had me up and down tekking pictures of de jumpsuits I see and sending dem to she and she ain' see one damn jumpsuit she like although I send she bout 20 pictures. Got me stanning up in de people stores holding up my phone in de air to get free WiFi and she in Barbados racking back like de Queen of Fucking Sheba telling me walk roun lil mo and see wuh other stores got in.

Anyhow, I wake up near one o'clock thirsty thirsty thirsty like I ain drink water fuh de day. I went downstairs to get a bottle of water from de fridge. When I get near de kitchen I hear something dat sound like moaning and I stop and listen but I ain hear it no more. When I get in de kitchen and turn on de light Melanie did pun de counter wid half of she clothes off and my father was only wearing he shirt and de rest of dem clothes did ... I cahn even talk bout it. Dem did kissing and moaning and my fadduh was talking bout he putting in work. I ain gaw tell you wuh did gine on. It was turrble and something that no child should ever see a parent doing. I scream out, Melanie scream out and my fadduh ask me wuh de hell I doing in de kitchen and start talking bout when yuh stannin' in people house yuh shun be roaming bout in de middle of de night. I tell he I did only want a bottle of water and now I scarred fuh life. No matter how I try I couldn't unsee wuh I see and when I went back in de bed I just couldn't fall sleep. The next morning I mek sure I scrub down dah counter before I put anything pun it. Nasty freaks. All now sometimes I does just get flashbacks out of nowhere like I got Post Traumatic Stress Disorder.

My father and Melanie promise that nothing so gine happen again so right now I actually pon de plane at Grantley Adams waiting fuh it to tek off fuh New York. I tired of Barbados. I tired of de men in Barbados. I tired of my muddah complaining bout everything. Plus, before I look round I gine be twenty-five and me and Trequon can be scotching at my muddah in a bedroom. Just last week a taxi-man dat live two gaps down from we get shoot when he did getting out he car one night. When I pass thru CircleSquare I does think how nice it would be fuh me and Trequon to live somewhey so one of dese days. I gotta try and do better fuh Trequon.

Tre tell me Trequon could stan' wid he and he muddah while I guh way. I know dem gine tek good care a Trequon and doan let he eat nuff corn curls nor nuh big lotta junk food. Tre muddah is a teacher so she does mek sure Trequon talk proper, not like some lil children talking bout tings like trewing gum and sounding brawling. The course gine be fuh six months and I gine miss Trequon real bad but Tre tell me he gine mek sure he video call me regular so I could see he and talk. Tre ask me if I sure I coming back and I tell he of course, cause Trequon hay. He tell me I might decide to stan in New York and then tell he I sending fuh Trequon but I tell he no, I cahn live nuhway but Barbados. When de course dun I coming back.

Trequon cry real bad as soon as I start to walk to de departure lounge and I had to beg Tre to cah he back home before he mek me cry more. I cry de whole a last night when I look at Trequon sleeping in bed but I like I still got tears left. Tre hold on pon me tight and tell me he gine miss me even though my ass annoying as hell. He catch me by surprise and he did smell so good my knees almost buckle.

Look, I gaw stop writing cause de plane lifting off. I gine look down at Barbados til is a dot in de ocean and I cahn see it nuh more.

#ComingBackSoon #EmpireStateofMind #BigLightsBigCity #PSTDSurvivor #StepUpInLife #VibrateHigher #CircleSquare #MhizzIzOverandOut

AUTHOR'S BIO

Claudia is an avid reader who has made good on a childhood promise to her- self to "one day" write a book. *CircleSquare*, her first collection of short stories, placed second in the 22nd Frank Collymore Literary Endowment Award in January2020.

Claudia is an attorney-at-law who loves music, dancing, and laughing at her own jokes. She spends her time overthinking and periodically working on several incomplete works of fiction which are always "almost finished".